Light as Air

Compass Boys, book 4

Mari Carr and Jayne Rylon

Dedication

To Dr. Lee, my very clever "storm-chasing" cousin at NOAA.
And to my daughter and her very dear friend from college, who was kind enough to loan me her beautiful name for my Rosalia.

ISBN: 978-1719414500

Editor: Kelli Collins

Cover artist: Jayne Rylon

Print formatting: Mari Carr

Prologue

Tap. Tap. Tap.
Sigh.
Tap. Tap. Tap.
Sigh.
"Change the radio, son. That song's getting old."

Doug Compton glanced up as Jake, one of the Compass Ranch hands, walked into the living room. Jake was more beloved surrogate grandfather than employee, but it didn't matter at the moment. Doug didn't want to see anybody.

He continued to tap the old cane his brother, James, had given him as a joke against his thigh-to-ankle cast.

Tap. Tap. Tap.

Jake came and stood behind him, taking a peek at the view outside the window.

Doug wasn't sure why he'd chosen this spot to set up camp for a lifelong sulk. Actually, he knew exactly why. It gave him a clear, unobstructed view of his saddle bronc, Buck.

Jake grunted behind him, and he waited for the older man to make some "life will get better" comment or give him hell for brooding and feeling sorry for himself.

Doug didn't want to hear it.

In one minute, every hope and dream for his future had been shattered, held together now by metal screws and plates. The only thing he had to look forward to the next few months was a shit-ton of rehab, and after that…

Well…there wasn't anything to look forward to after that.

Tap. Tap. Tap.

"If you've come to give me a pep talk, you can save your breath. Dad beat you to it yesterday."

"Since when have you known me to play cheerleader? Too old to shake a damn pom-pom."

Jake had a point—which meant he was here to ride herd on Doug's sorry hide.

"I don't wanna hear it's time to get my head out of my ass, either."

"Don't bother *me* if you want to wear your ass as a hat." Jake dropped down in the chair next to him.

Doug had spent the last two weeks in this very spot, his mother placing an ottoman in front of his seat so he could keep his broken leg propped up. When it became apparent after three days he'd settled in for the long haul, she'd moved the second chair over, creating a little sitting area that would allow friends and family members to "keep him company."

A few had tried, but his silence and sullen expression drove them away quick enough. Jake was made of sterner stuff.

"Really sucks about the leg."

Doug looked at Jake in surprise. No one, not one person, had acknowledged that yet. At least, not in his presence. He had no doubt they were saying it out of his earshot, worrying and stressing about him, but his family was nothing if not optimists. They always insisted there was a silver lining or a reason for shit happening. If there was one here, Doug didn't want to find it.

Since the day he was old enough to sit on a horse, he'd known what he wanted to be. He was born to live life just eight seconds at a time atop a raging bull, riding the circuit, king of the arena. In medieval times, he would have been a goddamned knight.

Now he was just plain old Doug, one in a long line of Compton men destined to live out his entire life on this ranch. No adventures, no glory, no buckle bunnies, no...nothing.

"Yeah," Doug said at last. "It sucks."

"Doctors say you can't ride Buck anymore? Even after the rehab?"

Doug nodded, recalled the moment he'd heard those words. After a few minutes of listening as the doctor explained the diminished strength he'd suffer in his left leg, and the unfortunate placement of the two breaks, and how metal screws wouldn't survive the continual beating of riding on a bucking bronc, the words had turned to white noise.

Doc had said a hell of a lot more, but Doug hadn't heard it. He let his parents digest the information while he sat there, stone-faced, fighting like the devil not to make an ass of himself by crying.

"I can't ride again. Rodeo is over for me."

Jake harrumphed. "Sucks," he repeated.

Doug was grateful to have someone to bitch to. Jake wasn't telling him to buck up or to look for a bright side. He looked as genuinely pissed off by this twist of fate as Doug.

"It's bullshit, is what it is," Doug added hotly.

The first time Doug had cussed within Jake's hearing, he'd only been eight, and the old hand had told him if he ever heard that kind of language from him again, he'd wash his mouth out with soap.

That threat had stuck, even after all these years—but only around Jake. When it was just Doug and his brother James around, and his cousins Austin and Bryant, he cussed a blue streak.

Now that he was sixteen, Jake didn't seem to mind. Instead, he just said, "Yep. Bullshit."

With that, the door was flung open. Doug spewed out all the anger and misery he'd been storing up the last few weeks. He'd spent day after day after day stewing silently, his fury building from sparking embers to raging wildfire. Until that moment, he'd been able to keep it contained, but Jake, with just a few words, managed to unleash it.

"Right?! What the fuck, man?" Doug shouted *to* Jake, not at him. "What the fuck do I do now? I'm not staying on this fucking ranch. I was supposed to ride the circuit."

Dream after broken dream fell out of him, along with four million "fucks" and "bullshits". It was a barrage of words filled with anger, injustice, unfairness and desolation.

Through it all, Jake let him rage, until finally, after several minutes, he started to run out of steam. "It was all I ever wanted. All..."

When he felt the anger turning to tears, he sucked in a deep breath and twisted his face away from Jake, unwilling to let him see the wetness in his eyes, the tracks as they spilled over and ran down his cheeks. He swiped at them with his sleeve, his chest burning from trying to hold it in.

Jake's hand landed on his shoulder. "Let it out, Doug. There's just so long a man can hold on to all that pain without burning alive."

It was the first time Jake had ever called him a man. Typically, he referred to him as "son" or "boy" or, on one of Doug's mischievous days, "son of a bitch."

But never a man.

The dam broke. Doug fell apart, the tears turning to sobs, all semblance of control gone. Everything streamed out of him in one long, loud rush. Through it all, Jake remained silent, though his hand never left Doug's shoulder. Jake let him know with that strong, comforting grip that he wasn't alone.

Finally, his voice hoarse from the shed tears, Doug said, "I was going to be somebody."

With that, Jake spoke, "Aren't you already somebody?"

Doug didn't know how to respond to that. Jake wasn't a fool. He knew what Doug meant by *being somebody*, knew that even while it might have seemed a childish dream when he was younger, Doug had put in the time, shed the blood and sweat and tears required to hone his skills, to master the art of riding the broncs. Doug had proven he had the grit and the drive to make his rodeo dream a reality.

And then, he got tossed. Not during an event, but here, on the ranch, by his own damn horse. A bee had stung Buck. It took both the beast and the rider by surprise and the horse bucked him off. Then, in a leaping, pained frenzy, Buck had come down on Doug's leg with both his hind ones, breaking the thigh and the shin and shattering the bones, before leaving Doug and his dreams in the dust cloud he'd kicked up.

"You know what I mean," Doug said quietly. Now that the storm had passed, he was feeling empty and exhausted.

"That's right. I do. But I'm gonna ask you again. Aren't you already somebody?"

Doug's shoulders slumped, then he rested his head on the back of the chair, a long sigh escaping out of him slowly, like air from a wilted balloon with a tiny pin prick.

"I don't know," Doug admitted. "I don't know *who* I am."

"Course you do. Say it."

Doug forced himself to look at the man. He'd already fallen apart in front of him, lost his shit and cried like a baby. If there'd been any pride left, he might've continued to avoid Jake's gaze, but Doug was completely out of it.

"What do you want me to say?"

"Tell me who you are."

Doug shrugged. "Right now? I'm Doug Compton. Just fucking Doug Compton."

Jake shook his head as if Doug was missing something obvious. "And what's wrong with that?"

"I know what you're trying to do, Jake."

Jake ignored him. "I've known you since you were a squalling baby in a shitty diaper. Saw you grow into a rough and tumble, rambunctious little boy with more energy than sense, constantly running around with scraped knees and torn jeans. I get it, Doug. I know how hard you've worked to make that rodeo dream a reality. I know what you put into it because I was in the stands cheering you on the whole time. It didn't turn out the way you thought, but that doesn't really change a goddamn thing. So tell me—who are you?"

The anger that had been consuming him for weeks was gone, washed out in that explosion of curses and tears. Without it there, scorching everything inside, he felt more clearheaded. Better able to think.

"I'm Doug Compton." His voice was stronger, more sure.

"Never seen him quit at anything, even when people told him something was impossible or the dream of a kid who didn't know better. You a quitter now?"

Doug shook his head. "No."

"Every man is tested. Every man has that moment when he has to decide who he is, deep down. Hell, you'll have more than one of those tests thrown your way in life. God knows I've had a few too many. This is your first. This one counts. Remember who you are and I figure you'll do just fine."

Doug couldn't reply, thanks to the big lump in his throat. Jake's advice struck a chord, hit the spot that made the difference, that pushed him around the corner. So instead, he simply nodded.

Jake pushed himself up, the movement a little slower, more difficult as he grew older. It was funny how Doug had never thought of the beloved man as old. Today, he looked...yeah...old, or maybe just tired. Either way, Doug didn't like it.

It was another wake-up call. Doug had lived the first sixteen years of his life assured that he'd get what he wanted *and* the people he loved would always be there.

Perhaps Jake was right. Doug was suddenly viewing the world through a man's eyes. It was a place where he would get knocked down. He would suffer pain and loss.

He would be tested.

Doug used the cane to rise, eschewing the nearby crutches. He didn't need them for this. He stood unsteadily, all his weight rested on his right leg as he reached his hand out, albeit the wrong one. Jake looked at it in surprise for a split second before taking it, the two of them shaking hands.

He was a man.

Doug wouldn't fail this test, wouldn't let Jake down.

More than that, he wouldn't let himself down.

Chapter One

Seven years later…

Doug stood outside the door, his knock drowned out by the shattering of glass. The sound justified Doug's purpose for being here. He was a man on a mission.

There was another loud thud and some cursing.

"Shit," he muttered, pounding his fist against the wood to be heard.

Thornton Joshua Nicholas, the third, opened the door, and Doug winced at the sight of his best friend's black eye.

Doug shook his head. "Jesus, man. Rough night?"

TJ gave him a tired grin. "Slim called me as I was leaving work, wanted Dad out of the bar. Thorn had other plans, mainly ones that included more whiskey and cussing out everyone within a five-mile radius. Fucker caught me in the eye with his elbow when I was trying to drag him out."

TJ's dad, Thorn, in addition to being a full-blown alcoholic, was the meanest drunk on the planet. Actually, the guy was a dick when he was sober, too. Doug figured that was how everyone in town wound up using the shortened version of his name. The man was prickly as a thorn, so it fit.

Thorn had always had alcoholic tendencies, but it had been more controlled when TJ's mom was alive. She'd been capable of doing what no one else could—keeping the man sober ninety-five percent of the time. The mean, bitter, full-time drunk had evolved slowly, starting when TJ's mom had died of cervical cancer when her son was eleven years old. Thorn had been holding his own until then, but with her passing, he fell off the wagon completely.

TJ had sat by his mom's bed and held her hand for weeks before she passed. And as much as Doug had loved TJ's sweet mother, he felt some resentment toward her these days. He wondered if she would have changed her last words if she'd known the curse she was leveling on her only child's head. She'd made TJ promise to always look after his dad, to take care of him.

TJ reasoned alcoholism was a disease just as much as cancer, and he had taken that promise to heart because there was nothing he wouldn't have given his mom to ease her suffering, her worry.

TJ had made and broken other promises in the time since, simply to keep that vow to his beloved mother. He'd never complained about his lot in life, rolling with the punches—literally and figuratively—taking care of his drunk father all through school, working part-time on Compass Ranch to help cover bills whenever his dad was out of work, something that happened more and more frequently as the years passed. By the time TJ graduated from high school, his dad's employment record was sporadic at best. Thorn worked just enough each week to cover his bar tab. Meanwhile, TJ's paycheck kept them in their house, with food in the fridge.

"Whodafuck at the door?" Thorn yelled, slurring his words together. Doug could hear the TV blasting, some sitcom, judging by the sound of canned laughter filtering out to them. Doug glanced over his friend's shoulder and caught sight of the man, kicked back in his recliner, bottle resting upright on his bloated stomach.

"Doug," TJ hollered back.

"Fucking Compton freaks," Thorn muttered, loud enough that it carried to them. "Should all be locked away from 'ciety."

TJ gave him a lopsided grimace, his face full of apology. "He got away from me this morning. Must have a new hiding place in the shed for his booze that I haven't found yet."

Violence wasn't a new thing in the Nicholas house. Sadly, it was an old thing in TJ's life.

TJ admitted once that the only reason he knew daddies didn't beat their sons' asses for breaking a dish or spilling a glass of milk was thanks to the time he spent on Compton Ranch with Doug's family.

Maybe because of that—or in addition to it—there was one thing Thorn Nicholas hated above all else in life.

The Comptons.

Doug and TJ had reasoned it out once and decided Thorn's hatred came from the fact that the Comptons had everything he didn't—a large, loving family, a successful business, even sobriety.

They also had no problem standing up to bullies, namely Thorn. After TJ showed up at the ranch late one night when he was in eighth grade with a bruised cheek and blood on his shirt from a split lip his dad put there,

Doug's father, Seth, and Uncle Silas paid a visit to Thorn.

Doug didn't have a clue what was said, but when they got back, Dad made two offers. The first was for TJ to come live with them. TJ refused, something that hadn't really surprised Dad or Doug. The second TJ's mom died, he'd taken over as his father's caregiver, something he wouldn't relinquish easily...if ever.

So Dad told TJ if Thorn ever laid another finger on him, he and Silas wanted to know. TJ made the promise, but Doug knew he'd broken it more than a few times, considering the blows he'd suffered his own fault for not dodging quick enough.

After Dad and Silas's visit, Thorn started referring to the whole family as freaks to anyone who would listen, claiming it was wrong for Silas to be married to Lucy and Colby. Then he added how disgusting it was for Hope to be with Wyatt and Clayton. And when Doug's cousin Bryant recently started dating Vaughn, the local tattoo artist, it merely inflamed Thorn's hatred anew as he spouted off about the Comptons being a bunch of fucking faggots.

Like a typical bully, Thorn never voiced his opinions in front of Silas or Wyatt or Vaughn, perfectly aware that all three of the men were more than capable of knocking his block off. Instead, he saved his venom for the other drunks at the bar or for TJ and Doug.

Not that his words didn't piss them off, too, but if they took him to task every time he said something, they'd be sporting permanent bruises on their fists and, as TJ had said more than once, "It wouldn't fix anything. Wouldn't change his mind or shut him up about it."

As such, they'd learned to let it slide.

"Pack a bag. You're done with this, Third."

Doug had dubbed him "Third" during their second-grade year, when they were practicing handwriting and TJ was struggling to spell out his moniker. The teacher had insisted he add "the third" to his name for some weird reason only educators ever seemed to understand.

Doug teased him about it at recess, calling him The Third. Damn if the name didn't stick and spread, with *The* dropped eventually as most of their school friends adopted it. Sometimes Doug felt kinda bad about that, but TJ claimed to think it was a hoot, so he didn't try too hard to break the habit.

"Bag for what?"

"Got you a job with that research crew I've been spending the last few springs with. Our second cameraman quit a couple weeks ago. We're in a bind. It's not great money, more internship than job, but you need to get out of this town— out of this house—for a while. Change of scenery will do you good."

TJ worked at the local lumberyard, a job they both knew he hated.

Doug rocked back on his heels, waiting for the inevitable response.

TJ didn't disappoint him. "You know I can't do that, Doug."

"Far as I can tell, you can. You're a twenty-three-year-old man, Third. You're dying on the vine in this town. I'm not asking you to leave forever. Just for a few weeks. Might encourage your dad to clean himself up."

Even as he said it, they both knew that was never going to happen.

On drunk days, Thorn cracked open the first bottle of cheap-ass whiskey with breakfast and he didn't stop drinking until he passed out, going through what TJ referred to as the Five Stages of Thorn. It started with him grumpily complaining about his morning hangover, sucking down Advil with the first glass of whiskey, moving through a brief spurt of maniacal happiness, followed by a dark depressed state that morphed into the irrational anger phase, and ended with the zombie pose he was clearly shifting toward right now as he stared at the TV, motionless, his eyelids closed into mere slits.

"He hit the fifth stage early today," Doug said, his tone more tired than angry. This conversation was one they'd been playing on repeat ever since high school graduation.

"Doug—" TJ started.

"I'm not leaving without you, man. I mean it. You're not your father's keeper."

TJ started to argue the point, but Doug cut him off.

"Fine. You think you are because of that damn promise to your mom, but you know what? He's an adult. You seriously plan to grow old here? This can't be the life you want for yourself."

"We can't always get what we want, Doug. You, of all people, should understand that. You didn't get what you wanted out of life, either."

TJ had shown up at the ranch just seconds after Jake had given Doug the talk that coaxed him out of his misery over his broken leg all those years ago. Doug could remember that visit like it happened yesterday, but not because it had changed the course of his professional life. It was because it had revealed something deep inside himself that he'd never seen before that day, something he'd never talked about aloud to another living soul, not Jake or Bryant or his brother James. Not even TJ.

17

Jake left after they shook hands, and Doug lowered himself back to the chair. He heard the older man talking briefly to someone at the front door. He recognized the voice and grimaced. His best friend, TJ, had stopped by every single day to check on him since the accident. And he'd been an asshole every time.

TJ stopped in the doorway.

"Hey," Doug said, giving him a friendly, if wary grin. TJ had every right to be pissed off at him.

"You done being a dick?"

Doug nodded. "Yeah."

"Good. Because I want to show you something." TJ claimed the chair Jake had just vacated, and Doug spotted the family's old video camera in his hands. "Borrowed this from your dad. We're going to start making videos."

For the better part of an hour, TJ laid out his plan for a journalism club at school as Doug listened, first skeptically, and then with genuine excitement.

He'd woken up this morning with no plan, nothing to look forward to and nothing but bitterness inside him. In the course of sixty minutes, Jake and TJ had changed all that.

"Why don't we move out to the front porch and start practicing with it?" Doug suggested, ready to leave his self-imposed chair prison.

He reached out, silently asking his friend for help to stand. TJ offered without hesitation. When Doug wobbled unsteadily, almost falling, TJ placed strong hands on his upper arms, keeping him upright. The position put their faces too close—and for a split second, he thought his best friend was going to kiss him.

And for that same split second, Doug realized he would let him.

The moment passed in the blink of an eye and Doug shook it off, blamed it on the pain meds. But the idea—no, the feeling—shook him.

Stuck with him all day, and in the weeks that followed.

TJ had spent a lot of time with Doug in the months after his accident. Finally out of his funk, Doug returned to his old self, doing most of the talking—as always—ready to discuss life and the future and new dreams. It wasn't until his rodeo plans were dashed that Doug realized TJ had never talked about his own hopes for the future. That was when he figured out TJ never let himself think very far ahead, his plans not stretching much beyond each day.

That knowledge had eaten at Doug for years, and he'd tried a million different times and ways to get his friend to let himself dream.

In the end, TJ said he was perfectly happy taking life one day at a time. Said it was the easiest way to avoid disappointment. Doug hadn't offered a response to that in the past because it was just as TJ said, after that broken leg, he *did* understand, even if he didn't agree.

Now Doug was ready for every argument. "Think about it, TJ. This is the perfect gig. It's only a short-time commitment, a vacation from our regular lives. Our chance to get out of this town and see a bit of the world."

TJ rolled his eyes. "I don't call driving all over the Midwest chasing tornadoes a vacation. It's the work of insane people."

Doug chuckled. "We don't just chase tornadoes. We're pretty fond of severe thunderstorms, too."

"You have issues," TJ said. "Besides, you can act like you can't wait to get out of this town, but we both know better. You'll be back for good eventually." He and Doug were Compton Pass boys through and through. Neither one of them would ever leave town forever. This place was too much a part of them. They may not have totally figured out their roles here, found their places, but they would.

"Fine. Then it's a chance for you to brush up on your video and photography skills. You have a great eye. It's a crime to waste it."

The two of them had indeed started a journalism club their junior year in high school, declaring they wanted to bring school news to the student body with their newfound camera skills. Neither one of them was short on charm, Doug's dad comparing them to used-car salesmen, proclaiming they could sell sunglasses to a blind man.

Fortunately, their new principal, Mrs. Watkins, had come from a big-city school where journalism was actually part of the curriculum, so she was pretty easy to persuade. She convinced the PTA to outfit them with a couple of used video cameras that were better than his dad's, one low-cost digital camera and a refurbished laptop computer. From there, CPSN—Compton Pass School News—was born, and the club was still going strong today.

TJ shook his head. "That was just something I did as a kid, man. To kill time until graduation. You were the real talent."

In that moment, Doug realized exactly how far TJ had fallen. Working the camera, as well as taking turns in front of it—interviewing their star football players, the Homecoming Queen and president of the Student Council—had been the highlight of their high school careers. It had gotten TJ out of the house and away from his dad, given him a chance to actually be a regular teenager for a while.

"That's bullshit and you know it."

TJ shrugged. "Doesn't matter. I haven't picked up a camera in years. Don't have a fancy degree."

Doug snorted. "I'd hardly call an associate's degree 'fancy.' And you should have taken those classes with me."

"Wasn't any money for that. Besides, we live in Compton Pass, Doug. Not Hollywood. What the hell good would that degree do me?"

"You could have been on the road with me these last few springs with the research team." Doug had begged TJ to join him at a nearby community college to study video with him the year after graduation. With rodeo off the table, Doug discovered a new direction in digital video production. He'd found the degree program and signed up with his family's blessing.

"Dad needed me close to home."

His friend's words drew Doug's gaze back to the black eye—and his anger sparked. "Pack the damn bag, TJ. You're not staying here."

"I can't. I'm sorry."

TJ was an easygoing guy, quiet, affable, but he wasn't a pushover. Doug didn't doubt that his friend had defended himself well against his dad all these years, despite the black eye he was sporting. Doug had been around to see more than a few of Thorn's violent outbursts. He would find some small offense, blow it out of proportion and start swinging. When he was younger, TJ had learned to move fast, to dodge, to get out of the house. He used to say it wasn't that hard to outrun an overweight, drunk, middle-aged man.

Now that he was older, he tended to stand his ground. Thorn would swing, TJ would dodge, then push back. He claimed it only took that one shove to remind his dad he was more than capable of kicking his ass these days.

The fact that Thorn landed an elbow bothered Doug. Because TJ was always on guard, always ready. Why had he lowered his defenses this time?

Doug had come here intent on winning the battle. He didn't like leaving TJ alone again.

Doug had traveled with the research team the past three springs during peak tornado season, filming the storms and the team's discussions as they analyzed the data. His family called him a storm chaser, and in some ways, he supposed that was true. However, most of their days were a hell of a lot less eventful, spent sitting around campgrounds, waiting for storms or in parking lots, releasing weather balloons ahead of oncoming bad weather. This year, they were heading out in the fall to study out-of-season tornadoes. There'd been a couple tornadoes in Illinois in November last year, and the team hoped to gather more data on the anomalies.

It was late August. They'd be gone until mid-December—something TJ didn't need to know at the moment—and if the weather predictions forecasting a turbulent autumn were true, Doug figured they wouldn't have a chance to come home between. Which served his purposes just fine. He wanted TJ away from Thorn for as long as he could manage.

Doug was chomping at the bit to get back to the team. He'd had to leave them a couple of weeks earlier than planned in May. Jake's unexpected death had taken him down harder than he'd anticipated, and he had remained at home, appreciating the months spent with his family. James and their cousins, Austin and

22

Bryant, had come home, and the Compass Boys had been together again. He'd needed that time as the four of them tried to get over the pain of losing their beloved mentor and friend.

Now, the research team was reuniting. Typically, he anticipated leaving to start another season with the same excitement as a twenty-year-old counting down the weeks 'til legal drinking age. But this time...he couldn't get the tightness in his chest to loosen up.

There was something different about TJ lately, and it wasn't a good change.

"I don't want to go without you," Doug admitted. He didn't say why, didn't want to admit that he was worried about him. His friend had grown continually quieter with each subsequent year, and now when he felt more ghost than human. He wanted his friend back. With Jake gone, and his brother and cousins all in love and shacking up with their girlfriends and—in Bryant's case—boyfriend, Doug felt the need to hold on to the only solid, reliable thing he had left.

TJ.

TJ gave him a funny look. "You don't need me there, Doug. You've got Rosalia, right?"

Doug grinned sheepishly. Rosalia Salvatore was the lead scientist on their research team, and Doug was crazy for her. He'd fallen head over ass for the woman the day he'd met her, back when she was a grad student working on her doctorate. She'd earned that degree a year ago and was currently a research scientist with NOAA, which meant nowadays, the storm study wasn't limited to short-term grant money, but had become a bona fide project without time constraints.

Sadly, Rosalia didn't seem to share the same fascination for *him*.

Yet.

While she jokingly referred to him as her work husband, she'd made it perfectly clear she wouldn't cross the line from colleagues and friends to lovers.

Bryant had introduced him to Rosalia when she'd mentioned her need for a skilled cameraman who would work for low pay. Rosalia was as personable as she was brilliant, so she'd secured a fairly large grant for her research during college, but most of that cash was used to pay for equipment.

As a side project, she'd begun sharing some of their storm-chaser videos on YouTube as a way to educate people on tornadoes. The videos went semi-viral, garnering enough views that Doug had convinced her to turn them into a proper show called *Lighter than Air*, with him serving as videographer and—at Rosalia's insistence—producer. They'd given the other guys in the research team gag titles as well, and when they scrolled at the end of every show, they always had a good laugh. The humorous ending didn't impact views, and now Rosalia was making some decent money from the show.

"I'm not sure I've got her. I'm not exactly her type. She's one of those super brains."

TJ tilted his head and looked at him like he was six eggs short of a dozen. "You're Doug Compton, man. Haven't seen the girl yet who can resist you."

Doug wished that was true, amused that his best friend had so much faith in his abilities to charm the ladies. "Yeah, right. Believe me, I'm not in Rosalia Salvatore's league. But I'm trying to get there."

He thought TJ would laugh at his joke, but he didn't.

"Why does this matter so much, Doug? You've gone away on these trips alone the last three springs. What's changed?"

TJ always saw through him, straight to the core. "My cousins and James are all partnered up, in love. Jake's gone." Even now, Doug couldn't say that without a hitch in his voice. He was only just now getting to the place where he could go almost a whole hour without remembering Jake was dead, then boom, it would sneak back into his mind and sucker punch him. "I just…I'm worried about you, and I'd feel a lot better if you were close to me."

Doug was concerned TJ would read more into his comment than he was comfortable with. His thoughts kept slipping back to that day by the window, to the look on TJ's face, to that almost kiss.

TJ snorted. "So this invitation is based on your need to protect me? I'm not a chick, bro. I can handle myself. It's just a black eye. You and I have both had them before."

Doug scowled. "It's not that. Did you ever think I'm fucking struggling and I need my best friend with me right now? These past few months have sucked, but when I'm with you…" Doug hadn't meant to say any of that. To confess how badly he was still hurting, how much he needed TJ.

TJ looked at him without replying for a solid minute.

"I'll grab my things. Give me fifteen."

Doug didn't bother to hide his smile. Jeez. He was an idiot. He should have known the surest way to secure TJ's agreement was to make it appear like the need was on the other side. TJ never said no to a friend in trouble.

"Want any help?"

TJ shook his head. "Don't have that much to pack. You got a sleeping bag for me?"

"Yeah. And we can share my four-man tent. You just need clothes and toiletries. What are you going to tell your dad?"

TJ glanced down the hall. Thorn was snoring loudly, his mouth hanging open. Then his hand lifted, gingerly touching his black eye. "Not a damn thing."

The response was completely out of character, and yet telling. TJ wasn't just taking this trip for Doug. He'd been right. His best friend was drowning here.

Doug threw his fist in the air, feeling victorious. "This is going to be one hell of an adventure."

TJ didn't bother to reply. Instead, he just walked away, shaking his head and muttering, "Only Doug Compton could get me to chase goddamn tornadoes."

Chapter Two

Rosalia leaned over the makeshift table set up outside the RV, tapping a few calculations on her laptop. This was her fourth season on the road, traveling all over the country, primarily the Midwest and South, trying to answer that age-old question of what caused tornadoes and how to predict their arrival.

Her team had broken camp at the end of May, all of them returning home for a few months. She'd returned to Pennsylvania, while Justin and Eric headed back to the apartment they shared just outside Boulder.

Rex, one of her two cameramen, had been chilling in Palm Springs for the summer with some friends. Then he'd found a new girlfriend—who'd lost her shit when he told her what he did for a living. He insisted on referring to himself as a storm chaser in hopes of impressing the women. That habit had backfired—for Rosalia, at least—when the jerk had emailed her a couple weeks ago to quit at the request of his "true love," who couldn't stand to know he was putting himself in danger.

Knowing Rex, he'd be begging to return come the end of September.

Doug had been gone longer, returning home earlier after the unexpected death of a man he called his surrogate grandfather. He had talked about Jake countless times, telling so many stories about the man, she felt like she'd known him.

Rosalia didn't want to admit, even to herself, that those two weeks spent on the road without him weren't nearly as much fun. The past few years, traveling with this team, had been some of the best times of her life, and Doug, the charming comedian, was typically at the center of it all.

She'd had a brief moment of panic a few hours ago when she got an email from him that simply said "Change of plans" in the subject heading. She'd opened the email fearing he had quit as well. Losing him as a cameraman would be tough...but not having him around for all the reasons that had nothing to do with science would be much worse. She always joked, calling him her work husband, but that wasn't too far from the truth.

She could confide in him when the research stalled or the data didn't make sense. Rosalia knew he probably didn't understand a tenth of the stuff she was talking about, but he was an amazing listener, and even without the scientific knowledge, he had a strong sense of logic combined with common sense. Which, in a lot of ways, made him way smarter than her, and she wasn't too proud to admit it. He was the perfect counterbalance to her bookishness.

Doug reminded her of her brothers, though she suspected he wouldn't enjoy that comparison. He'd made a comment once about her hastiness in friend-zoning him three minutes after they'd met. She *had* done that, but not for the reasons he might think.

She'd grown up in Philly with her large Italian family—she was the only daughter amongst six brothers—working part-time in her parents' restaurant during summer breaks, holidays and weekends. She'd started hostessing, bussing tables, and serving in high school, and had returned to do the same throughout college as well.

There were some deep fundamental similarities between her boisterous, overprotective brothers and Doug. She'd always seen the caring, attentive way her brothers looked at their girlfriends, and she wanted that same thing in her own future relationships. Wanted to be adored and—even though it wasn't the most feminist of feelings—coddled and protected.

Doug Compton was sex-on-a-stick hot, with an easygoing country-boy charm that was pretty hard to resist. And she suspected—because of her *all work, no play* policy—he restrained himself when it came to hovering, fighting the instincts that told him to get her out of the storm paths.

Rosalia wondered what would happen if she let him off his leash and gave him the green light on a more intimate relationship.

So far, she'd managed to keep him tethered—for a couple of pretty simple reasons. One, they worked together, and she had always felt this ingrained need to maintain a high level of professionalism. Secondly, she was contrary, and something told her Doug was used to women falling madly in love with him at one glance. She refused to succumb…easily.

She shook that thought away.

She wasn't succumbing to anything.

At all.

But just in case, she closed her eyes and sent up a silent prayer for strength. June had been a tough month for her, and she was still feeling off-balance, vulnerable, sad.

Her doctor had found a large cyst in one of her ovaries; actually, it was a *huge* cyst. The solution had been an oophorectomy, where the surgeon removed the affected ovary using a laparoscope. The surgery had been a success, and for a few days, her mother had bundled her up under cozy blankets and waited on her hand and foot. That part had been sort of wonderful.

The problem was the weeks and months since. She was a creature of habit and a workaholic. Those two attributes had determined her lifestyle for as long as she could remember. The cancer scare frightened that out of her, and she'd spent too much time lately focusing on regrets. As it turned out, she had a ton of them...and the main one involved her foolish decision to put Doug in the friend zone.

Rosalia shut the bad feelings away. She had promised herself that she'd lock up those emotions when she hit the road again. She was back in her environment and ready to start the research, to reunite with her team...with Doug.

Mercifully, Doug's email about changing his plans had been good news. He was returning today with another cameraman in tow. Someone named JT or JR or some combination of letters. She'd been trying, unsuccessfully, to find a second cameraman since Rex quit on her. After all, it wasn't like she had a ton of money to offer anyone, and the work wasn't for the weak-willed. While they always kept a safe distance from the storms and took precautions, there weren't a lot of people who wanted to be out in the elements while a tornado raged close by.

The sound of a vehicle approaching caught her attention and she smiled, waving when Justin and Eric came into view, towing their pop-up camper behind them. They parked beside her, and the next hour passed in a whirlwind as she helped them set up their camper. Like her, they were science majors in the same field. While she'd already earned her doctorate, Justin and Eric were using this field research as part of their graduate studies.

The three of them had just gotten a blaze going in the fire pit and settled in their chairs with beers in hand, when an old truck rumbled down the lane past all the lots in the fairly empty campsite. It was a weekday, and schools were back in session after the summer break. The only fellow campers in this section of the campground were a retired couple in a swanky RV quite a few sites away. The main reason Rosalia had picked this site was because it was secluded.

Doug and Justin were both fun guys who could get a little loud as they tried to one-up each other on tall tales. The last thing she wanted was to have someone complain about them…again. It had happened too many times in the past, so she'd wised up. Learned to find them the most private spots she could manage. She was actually starting to fear their pictures were hanging up in state park check-in stations around the country. Justin lost all control of the volume after a few PBRs.

Rosalia recognized the truck and smiled as she stood up, trying to calm the sudden racing of her heart when she caught sight of Doug's face behind the wheel. He was wearing the cowboy hat that never seemed to leave his head, and she braced herself to look into those chocolate-colored eyes after so many months apart.

Doug parked the truck and stepped out. Rosalia wasn't sure what it was about a man in well-worn, faded blue jeans, work boots and a tight T-shirt that got her all hot and bothered, but whatever the appeal, Doug had it in spades.

She wasn't surprised when he walked right over to her, picked her up and swung her around. He tended to touch her whenever he had the opportunity, putting his arm around her when they hiked over rocky terrain, or taking her hand if they found themselves walking after dark.

Then he gave her a quick kiss on the cheek. "There's my best girl."

She narrowed her eyes, pretending to be annoyed so she didn't have to acknowledge the effect his sexy voice had on her best girl parts. Her nipples were budding, and it sure as hell wasn't because it was cold outside. "Let's revise to make that statement accurate. I'm not yours and I'm not a girl."

Doug didn't bother to pretend he was sorry. Instead, he let his gaze drop lower to her breasts in a playful ogle. She resisted the urge to cross her arms, afraid he'd see his effect on her firsthand. "You're right about the girl thing. You're all woman."

She smacked him on the shoulder. "I thought absence was supposed to make the heart grow fonder." She glanced over at Justin with a wink. "I feel absolutely nothing."

Justin and Eric laughed as Justin muttered, "Here we go again. It's time for the Rosie and Doug Show."

Rosalia noticed Doug's friend for the first time— and just barely restrained her groan.

Fuck.

There were two of them.

The new man was six-foot-something of pure muscle, dirty-blond hair, with a chiseled jaw and rugged face that should be on billboards.

He wore sunglasses, which left her longing to drag them off him so she could see if his eyes were as amazing as the rest of him. After all, it wasn't like he needed them for shade. The sun had set and dusk fallen. She was a sucker for eyes, proclaiming she could learn so much about a person simply by looking into them.

Doug's eyes practically twinkled with humor and kindness. The second she'd seen him, and looked into those brown eyes, she'd known he was going to become someone very important in her life. And she hadn't been wrong. If she sat down to create a list of the best friends she'd ever had in her lifetime, Doug would be in the top five. Hell, he'd be top three.

"Rosie, this is my friend, TJ Nicholas. The new cameraman I found us. TJ, this is Rosalia Salvatore, prettiest scientist in the country. No," he corrected. "The world."

TJ stepped closer, tugging off his sunglasses as he reached out to shake her hand. She slid her hand in his, then gasped softly at her first up-close look of his face.

He was sporting a black eye—but it wasn't the dark bruise that caused her reaction. His eyes were pale blue, stormy, distant.

Her grandmother had always told her that eyes were the mirror to the soul, and Rosalia was a firm believer. TJ's called out to her on an almost primal level. She saw a lonely, scared boy, and it took everything she had not to turn the handshake into a hug, to pull him toward her, to comfort him.

TJ gave her a crooked grin and made a joke about the black eye, promising he wasn't the brawling type. She'd half expected him to use the old "I walked into a door" line, but Doug saved him from having to lie.

"You should see the other guy."

Rosalia knew there was a story behind the shiner. She also knew neither man was going to tell it to her.

"It's nice to meet you, TJ. I can't tell you how happy I am you could join the team. We were starting to get a bit desperate. While Doug's more than capable, he just can't capture all the footage we need on his own, both for the research and the show."

"Happy to help out. Though I'll warn you, my skills are a bit rusty."

TJ had a deep-voiced, slow country drawl that had Rosalia's pussy clenching. Her hormones were so out of whack right now. That had to be the reason for her wet-panty reaction to these two.

Right?

Then she glanced at Justin and Eric, and realized the two nerdy scientists did absolutely zilch for her. So...she didn't know what to blame her over-the-top arousal on.

"I hope it doesn't uproot your everyday life too much. I realize being gone until mid-December can be an imposition. Are you a rancher like Doug?"

TJ glanced at Doug, and she sensed an air of surprise. "Mid-December, huh?"

Doug shrugged, obviously caught in some untruth, and Rosalia sighed. Doug had lied about the length of the gig. She didn't want to have to find another cameraman at this late date, but more than that, she really didn't want TJ to leave. She'd never felt such an intense pull toward a man she'd just met. It was slightly unnerving.

Finally, TJ looked her way again. "I'm not a rancher, Rosalia. I didn't leave anything behind that won't be there when I get back."

She would have sighed with relief if all the breath hadn't vanished from her lungs at the sound of her name rolling off his lips in that delicious tone. Everyone else on the team called her Rosie, the nickname that she'd carried since the cradle. Very few people called her Rosalia. Actually, just one. Her grandmother.

And now, TJ.

The sky rumbled and she glanced up. Storm clouds had formed. Not that she was surprised by that. After a long drought this summer, the weather had finally broken, giving the scorched earth a big drink of water. It had been raining off and on for days. Tonight promised to offer up a fairly decent downpour.

"Looks like we're going to get wet," TJ muttered. "We better set up the tent. Hope you've got a good tarp, Doug."

TJ and Doug started studying the trees, looking for a spot that would provide the most cover from the rain.

"Tell you what," Rosalia said, her words flying out without consulting her brain. "Why don't you keep your gear packed up tonight. It's already getting dark. The dining booth in my RV doubles as a bed. I'll push the seats down and sleep there, and you two can sack out in my bed tonight. Nothing worse than starting a trip with a wet tent and sleeping bags. The sun's not expected to make an appearance again for a few days, so your stuff will be damp until the weekend without some heat to dry it out."

TJ and Doug both started to shake their heads, but she didn't give them a chance to reject the idea.

"Great," she said, "So it's settled."

"Rosie," Doug started.

She shot him a look, then a smile. "I'm the boss, Doug. Remember?"

He rolled his eyes. "That didn't take long. Justin and I didn't even have time to make up the pool or place bets on when you'd pull the boss card."

"Told you we should have set it up through email," Justin said, slapping Doug on the shoulder as he shook his head regretfully over the missed opportunity to wager.

She laughed. "Grab your bags. I'll start moving the stuff inside that we don't want getting wet."

Justin walked over to put out the bonfire. "So much for dinner. Me and Eric might run out for a while, see if we can find a fast-food joint nearby. I'd kill for a Whopper with cheese and some fries right now. You all want anything?"

Rosalia—the boss—answered for them. "No thanks. I've got two-thirds of a pan of lasagna my mother packed up for me when I got on the road a couple days ago. Plenty for the three of us if you guys want to share."

Doug rubbed his hands together in excited anticipation. "Your mom's lasagna? I'm in."

TJ nodded. "Nice of you to share your supper, Rosalia."

The wind was picking up, and while she knew there was a sudden chill in the air, it wasn't touching her overheated state. She felt downright feverish.

TJ and Doug continued securing the campsite after Justin and Eric left, while Rosalia went into the RV to start heating up their dinner. Once everything was under cover or tucked away inside the vehicles, the guys joined her.

She pointed to the wine on the counter. "Grab that bottle of red, Doug, and pour us all a glass."

The RV was on loan from her oldest brother. When it was just her, the vehicle felt almost too big. The same didn't hold true when TJ and Doug came inside. They were large, well-built men, both a few inches over six feet, with broad shoulders and muscular arms that screamed of hard work. She laughed when they tried to push themselves into the booth in the dining area, their knees knocking against each other under the table as they clamored for space.

"Might be easier for you two if you turned the driver and passenger seats around and ate with your plates on your laps."

While TJ seemed to think that was a good idea, Doug looked scandalized. "Not eat at the table?" He shook his head. "Dinnertime is sacred in my house. We all sit at the table, with no technology, and we talk...like civilized human beings."

"Jesus," TJ muttered. "You sounded exactly like your dad there. Never thought I'd hear you channeling Seth Compton."

Rosalia laughed as she tried to imagine her large family making that same dining-room-table attempt night after night. Actually, it was rare for her entire family to be home for dinner. They owned a restaurant, which meant that was rush hour. Most of her meals growing up had been consumed in the restaurant's kitchen, standing at the counter during her break, shoveling in whatever that night's special was.

"I like that tradition. Sounds nice," Rosalia said.

TJ chuckled. "Yeah. It is, actually. I enjoy eating dinner with your parents, Doug. Your mom always has crescent rolls with real butter on the table. Damn, I love those things."

"Your family's not big on the dinnertime traditions, TJ?" Rosalia asked, very curious about the man Doug called his best friend. Based on her first impression, she'd say the two of them were as different as night and day. Doug was an open book with a personality as big and bright as the sun. TJ seemed quieter, the type to play his cards close to his chest.

"No. It's just me and my dad. Thorn's culinary talents begin and end with Hungry Man microwave dinners. Think the directions on the box say you're supposed to eat them in front of the TV. Might even be the law."

Doug laughed, but she crinkled her nose. "You poor thing. Those meals are terrible."

TJ lifted one shoulder. "They're not that bad. Food is really just fuel anyway."

Rosalia was horrified. "Just fuel?"

Doug shook his head. "Oh man. Now you've done it."

"Done what?" TJ's forehead creased in concern.

Rosalia was Italian, and she'd been raised right. "Food is magic. Food is life. Food is…everything."

TJ's expression still didn't clear, so she continued to explain.

"Let me put it this way. Never—ever—spout that craziness in front of an Italian, and definitely no one in my family. It just makes it clear you've never had good food. But," she said, dipping out a large helping of her mother's homemade lasagna, "tasting is believing." She sliced a piece of garlic bread as well, recalling TJ's confession about loving the crescent rolls, and added it to the plate.

"Voila," she said, placing it on the table in front of TJ and handing him a fork.

Then she did the same for Doug, dipping out her own plate last, before scooching into the booth next him.

She picked up her fork, but didn't scoop up a bite of food. Her gaze was firmly glued to TJ's face as he put the first forkful into his mouth.

Rosalia didn't bother to hide her gloat when his eyes closed in absolute ecstasy.

"Holy sh…" he murmured, quickly taking another bite. He'd consumed three more, as well as half of the buttery, crispy garlic bread, before he managed to emerge from his bliss. He looked like he was quickly drifting toward a food coma.

He caught her watching him and grinned. There was something very sexy about TJ Nicholas's smile.

"Okay. I get it."

Doug snickered. "Not even going to put up a fight? Damn, man. Way to cave like a house of cards."

TJ didn't take his eyes off her, and Rosalia tried to ignore the blush his intense gaze enflamed. "No point fighting when I'm wrong. This is the best thing I've ever eaten."

"I'm telling my mom you said that, Third," Doug teased. "You made the same comment about her meatloaf."

TJ narrowed his eyes. "Snitches get stitches."

Suddenly, Rosalia realized who TJ was. Like Jake, Doug had told countless stories about his best friend, Third. She hadn't made the connection that TJ was Third until that moment.

"Third?" Rosalia had always wondered about the strange name, but never thought to ask where it came from.

"Doug's nickname for me," TJ explained.

"Compton Pass's nickname for him," Doug added.

"Thanks to you," TJ muttered as he continued shoveling in the lasagna. His clear enjoyment made her want to hand him her plate as well, just so she could continue to listen to his low groans of bliss.

From his mild response, Rosalia didn't get the sense TJ minded the odd moniker. "What's it stand for? Were you third baseman in little league or something?"

TJ put his fork down and wiped his mouth. "Nothing that interesting. I'm at the tail end of an unimpressive legacy. Thornton Joshua Nicholas, the third. Josh Nicholas, my grandfather, skipped over the first name, opting to go by the middle. He passed the whole name along to my dad three seconds after he was born and five seconds before he split for good. Thorn, the second, adopted the part of the name that fits him best. Prickly bastard. Which leaves me, TJ, the third."

Rosalia tried to match the words to the tone, but she couldn't make them fit. TJ spouted off his family's history with the same emotion her grandmother might use when repeating a recipe to a friend over the phone.

"They saved the best for last," Doug said easily, using the typical kind, supportive words she would have expected from him.

TJ gave his friend a grateful, if unconvinced nod. "Thanks, Doug. So...I hear you're an Internet star, Rosalia."

Rosalia grinned, sorry that TJ had found a way to change the subject.

But maybe it was for the best. It wasn't that she didn't want to learn more about TJ—God, she was suffering from an almost unnatural fascination with the man—but she could tell it bothered him to talk about himself. His eyes had darkened, cast with shadows, when he talked about his family.

They were going to be together—in close proximity—for the next four months. While that didn't sound like a lot, she'd learned from previous research trips, time spent around a campfire, outside in the fresh air, created a sort of break from reality, a circle of trust and truth. It was like summer camp.

"Not sure I'd say star. I have a little YouTube channel that—"

"Little?" Doug interjected. "I don't call a hundred thousand followers a little channel."

She laughed. Doug was her biggest fan and loudest supporter. When she'd told him about the few weather videos she'd uploaded onto YouTube their first spring together, he'd convinced her to put some more time and effort into them, proclaiming storm chasing one of those things viewers would want to see. She'd renovated her channel, giving it the title *Light as Air*, and started taking more care to make her videos look professional.

Actually, it was Doug who did the polishing and editing. And while the subject matter sounded fascinating, she wasn't going for the sensational as much as the educational, and apparently, that was what set her apart from the crowd.

She took the time to explain the science behind the storms they filmed. It caught the attention of teachers across the country, who were now using her videos in their Earth Science classrooms. When she learned about that, she'd started including questions for discussion and educational links at the end, to enhance the videos' instructional value.

She was actually shocked when her number of followers skyrocketed enough that she started earning money for her efforts. Money she put into adding a second cameraman to the crew. Rex, and now TJ were paid with the YouTube windfall.

"That channel wouldn't be where it is today without your influence, Doug."

TJ smiled, and she realized how close these guys really were. A compliment paid to one seemed to genuinely please the other.

Doug tried to dismiss her words, but she wouldn't let him. "Seriously. Your camerawork and video editing is stellar." She looked at TJ. "I taped the original shows with my phone."

TJ feigned a wince, then laughed. "Doug is great behind the camera. Although he's pretty cool in front of it, too."

"In front?" she asked.

For the next hour, they polished off the first and second bottles of wine as the guys told her all about CPSN.

If anyone had asked, Rosalia would have said there was very little she didn't know about Doug. Tonight, she was proven wrong. TJ had a much deeper, longer, richer history with her friend, and it was fun to hear Doug's stories from someone else's perspective. Doug was too self-effacing, too unpretentious to ever really talk too seriously about himself.

Hearing his stories told by his best friend from kindergarten shed a spotlight on how little she knew, but how right she'd been all these years to adore the man.

Between the wine and the company of two of the sexiest men she'd ever known, Rosalia was hard-pressed not to strip off some clothes. As it was, she stood at one point and picked up a paper plate to fan herself.

"Hot?" Doug asked, glancing around as if he'd crack a window. Unfortunately, the rain was still coming down hard and the wind had picked up.

"I'm fine," she assured him. "Just the wine, *dear*." She emphasized the last word. "Doug is the perfect work husband. Always taking care of me."

Doug sighed. "We could take the word 'work' out of that sentence if you would just go ahead and admit you're madly in love with me."

"Gonna put a ring on it, huh?" she teased, this routine part of what Justin called the Rosie and Doug Show.

"In a New York minute."

Rosalia started to laugh, but the sound died on her lips. There was something different in Doug's tone. Or maybe it was the same tone as always, but she was just hearing it for the first time. He sounded…earnest.

She blinked a few times, forgetting the rest of the joke, unable to come back with some witty shoot-down.

Headlights hit the wall and she glanced out the window, feeling relieved to be saved.

And disappointed.

"Justin and Eric are back."

Doug rose, coming to stand behind her. "Looks like they're heading straight to their camper."

She looked at her phone. "No wonder. It's nearly midnight. What the heck did they get up to?"

"Probably found a bar."

"Probably," she agreed. "Maybe we should turn in, too. All of us put in quite a few hours today driving here."

"Good idea." TJ stood as well, and Rosalia was tempted to fan herself once more. With both of them next to her in the confined space, her fantasies went wild. "Listen, Rosalia. We're not taking your bed. Doug can sack out on that booth and I'll sleep here on the floor."

She shook her head. "Nope. Absolutely not. No one's sleeping on the floor."

TJ frowned, ready to continue the fight, but Doug chuckled.

"That's her boss voice."

"What's that mean?" TJ asked.

"It means you won't win in a fight with me," she said, unoffended by Doug's joke. She was used to the guys giving her shit for her tendency to be a bit of a control freak.

TJ didn't look like he was willing to give in, but she didn't give him the chance. "I've slept on the bed out here plenty of times before. It's perfectly comfortable. So go on."

Doug gave her a quick, friendly hug and kiss on the top of her head that sent her thoughts down a very racy road before he started toward the bedroom. "Next time it rains, I say we shake up the sleeping arrangements. Just to keep things interesting and fun. We can practice that future-wife-and-husband thing."

She narrowed her eyes. "Next time, I'll make you sleep in the tent in that downpour."

He waved his hand to let her know he'd heard the joke and let it bounce right off him.

"Is that the research-team equivalent of making a man sleep on the couch?" TJ asked with a grin.

She nodded. "Yeah. Something like that."

"Thank you for dinner, Rosalia."

"You can call me Rosie. Everyone else does."

"I know. But I'm not everyone else."

She sucked in a breath, not sure if any air got to her lungs. She was suddenly light-headed. While Doug made her feel pretty and adored, TJ made her hot and bothered...in a very lonely, never-been-touched-before place.

"If you're too uncomfortable, just wake us up and we'll move out here. It's your RV and your bed, after all. I've slept in worse places than the floor of a camper or a tent in the rain, so don't let that worry you."

TJ's words fueled her curiosity about him even more.

Then he followed the direction Doug had gone, disappearing into the bedroom.

If she was a better woman, she would have looked away and not ogled his gorgeous ass in those tight blue jeans the whole time.

"Dammit," she mumbled. There was too much testosterone in this RV, and she wasn't in the right frame of mind to combat it.

It had been hard enough to control her overheated fantasies when it was just Doug with the research team. With TJ in the picture...

She was starting to regret offering to share her RV. How the hell was she supposed to sleep with those two just a few feet away?

It was going to be a long night.

No. It was going to be a long fall.

Chapter Three

Doug sat sprawled out, beer in hand, and sighed contently. It was times like these when he considered himself the luckiest bastard on earth. He was camped out by a warm fire on a clear night with his best friends and not a care in the world.

He'd always loved the time he spent with the research team each spring, but this time was different, better. Having TJ along was taking a lot of anxiety away. He'd always worried about his friend, alone in the ramshackle house he shared with his dad. While he knew TJ was capable of taking care of himself, he didn't like thinking that he always had to be on guard or that he might suffer any loneliness. There was just so long a man could keep that up before he ran out of steam.

TJ's black eye a couple weeks earlier seemed to indicate that his strength had been waning.

TJ was a different man away from Compton Pass, more relaxed, more like the boy he'd been in high school...so Doug hadn't bothered to tell him about the phone call from his father earlier today.

Apparently, Thorn had taken a swing at Doug's uncle Sawyer, the sheriff of Compton Pass, when he'd arrested him for being drunk in public earlier in the week. Thorn had just spent the last few nights in jail. Given the fact no one from home had informed Doug until today—when Thorn was released—it was obvious his family was hoping to give TJ a break from the hell that was his reality for as long as possible as well.

It had been on the tip of his tongue to tell TJ, but then he'd caught a glimpse of his friend laughing and swapping stories with Justin, and Doug had shut his mouth, unwilling to ruin this chance for TJ. He hadn't mentioned Thorn since their first night here, and Doug would do anything necessary to keep it that way.

Out of sight. Out of mind.

He wasn't sure what had caused TJ to regress to the quieter, sadder version of himself these last couple of years, but seeing *this* TJ, the one who smiled and talked, was a welcome relief.

There was country music playing softly as they all sat together, talking about a whole lot of nothing. Justin was munching on his third s'more like a freaking twelve-year-old at summer camp. They teased him about his obsession with making the sweet snack nearly every single night, but that also didn't stop the rest of them from partaking as well.

"I'm going in for the night," Eric said. "Thursday-night football. Gonna stream it on my iPad while I lay in bed."

"Who's playing?" Justin asked.

"Seahawks and Packers."

"Oooo. Can I watch too?" Justin was already up and out of his chair, gathering his s'mores makings.

"Sure."

Doug watched the two guys disappear into the pop-up camper they shared. Neither he, Rosalia nor TJ moved.

"I don't want to go in yet," Rosalia said quietly.

"Me either." TJ took a sip of his beer. "Too comfortable here. I like watching the fire."

Doug felt the same way. He wasn't sure what it was about a campfire that soaked into his soul and made him feel peaceful.

The longer they stayed here, the more Doug could forget the rest of the world existed. It was one of the reasons he'd wanted TJ to come along so badly.

If anyone needed to forget about life for a while, it was TJ.

"Die a Happy Man" came on the radio and Rosalia smiled. "I love Thomas Rhett. He is such a hottie."

"I like slow country songs. Reminds me of high school prom," TJ said. "Doug and I double-dated for our senior one."

Doug picked up the story. "Took the Pearson twins. Hannah and Heather."

Rosalia laughed. "Why does this story not surprise me? And why do parents always feel the need to give twins names that start with the same letter or that rhyme?"

Doug shrugged. "One of the great mysteries of life."

"Who did you go to prom with, Rosalia?" TJ asked.

Doug had a feeling he knew what Rosalia's response would be before she gave it. Over the past few years, he'd learned she had been a loner in school, super smart and shy. She had told him once that she'd started working in the family restaurant in order to save money for college. With seven kids in the home, her family simply didn't have the funds to send her to any university. So a fourteen-year-old Rosalia took it upon herself to set up the college fund, dividing her time between work and school, saving every penny for her future.

"I didn't go."

TJ frowned. "Why not? Because I know there's no way in hell you weren't asked."

Rosalia blushed.

Doug had noticed her pink-cheeked reaction to TJ ever since the first night. He tried to ignore it, tried to push away the thought that the woman he was crazy about was interested in his best friend.

"I was asked by one boy. But it was more along the lines of a 'since neither one of us has anyone to go with, we might as well go with each other' invitation. I said no. Saturday nights are the busiest at the restaurant, and I couldn't see wasting so much money on a dress I'd only wear one time."

Typical Rosalia response. She was always too practical, an old soul who never seemed to succumb to the things most girls considered a rite of passage.

"What about other dances?" TJ persisted.

She shrugged one shoulder, her silence answering.

TJ leaned forward. "Didn't you *ever* go to a dance before?"

Rosalia shook her head, and Doug noticed the same sadness he'd been seeing the last two weeks creep back into her eyes. There was something going on with her, but he hadn't known how to ask her, or even what to ask. On the surface, she was the same old Rosie. It was only on occasion that he caught these glimpses or got this feeling something was bothering her.

He kept dismissing the thought because Rosalia told him everything when they were on the road and even when they were off, the two of them emailing and calling several times a week when they were apart. He was her shoulder, and she was his. If something was up, she'd tell him.

He hoped.

When her somberness persisted, Doug pushed himself out of the chair. "Well, then we'll just have to take you to your first dance tonight."

Rosalia tilted her head. "What dance?"

"The campfire dance. It's all the rage these days. Way more popular than prom or homecoming."

She laughed when he held out his hand, letting him pull her up and into his arms. His body reacted before his brain could kick in.

His cock thickened and every muscle tightened with need. She smelled like Hershey chocolate and woodsmoke, and he breathed her in as they swayed in time to the song.

Doug wasn't sure what he expected Rosalia's reaction to his impromptu dance to be, but it was pretty much anything *other* than what she did.

She had resisted his flirting throughout the last three trips, claiming they were colleagues and that was a relationship line she'd never cross.

That didn't feel like the case right now.

Rosalia let him pull her close, her body flush to his, her breasts crushed against his chest. She pressed her cheek to his, every now and again moving it slightly, as if she couldn't resist caressing his face with hers.

There wasn't an inch between them, and her arms held him tightly.

Doug moved his hands from her waist to her back, his fingers lightly stroking along her spine.

While his friend remained quiet, Doug could feel the weight of TJ's gaze on them. He chanced a look over—and his heart squeezed almost painfully at the sight of the naked desire on TJ's face.

TJ wanted Rosalia. That much was obvious. But there was something else smoldering there that Doug was struggling to reconcile.

Because TJ wasn't looking at just Rosalia. He was looking at *him*, too.

The song ended, but Doug didn't notice until Rosalia released him, taking a step back. "Thanks for the dance, Doug. It was really nice."

It took everything he had not to tug her back into his arms—music or not. He wanted to kiss her. No. He wanted to do a hell of a lot more than that.

He wanted her naked, under him. Wanted to bury himself deep inside her wet heat, take her hard and fast, and then take her again.

And…he wanted TJ there with them.

Doug dropped his arms, freeing her as the unexpected, forbidden dream drifted through his mind.

Doug had come to grips a long time ago with the fact that his family didn't follow the same rules when it came to falling in love.

He'd been nearly eight before he realized that his uncle Silas's marriage to Colby and Lucy wasn't something lots of people did. Up until then, he'd always figured marriage was between two or three people who loved each other, and it didn't matter if a man fell for a woman or another man.

When Hope had fallen for both Wyatt and Clayton, the family had accepted the union without a blink. And he'd figured out in middle school that Bryant was into guys, not girls, and it hadn't felt weird or wrong to him.

Love is love. No matter what.

His mother, Jody, had recited those words to him countless times over the years, and he'd taken them to heart, believed them as gospel truth.

But TJ and Rosalia hadn't been raised by Comptons. They were raised in a society that said marriage was best between two people, and for the even *less* open-minded in the world, those two people had to include one man and one woman.

"Mind if I take a turn?"

Doug jerked, surprised to hear TJ's voice right behind him.

"Of course not." Doug stepped aside and watched as his best friend took Rosalia into his arms, the two of them dancing to "Marry Me," as the station did a two-fer of Thomas Rhett songs.

He backed away, dropping down into his chair, trying to calm his racing heart. His thoughts were taking him somewhere he couldn't go in reality.

Doug forced himself to look away from them, studying the fire, fighting to find enough air to fill his lungs.

His eyes betrayed him, continually drifting back to the sight of TJ and Rosalia dancing. She wasn't holding him as tightly, but they were still close. TJ didn't have the benefit of a long friendship with her. The two of them were essentially strangers. But that didn't seem to matter as they danced.

TJ wasn't doing a very good job, trying to hide his feelings. He was looking down at her as if she hung the moon. Something that wasn't lost on Rosalia, who kept sneaking glances upward, her cheeks flushed. Every time she lifted her face, their lips were mere inches apart.

What would Doug do if they kissed?

The question rambled round and round in his brain. Would he walk away? Or move closer and join in? And how would they respond if he did?

He looked away once more, and this time he closed his eyes.

Doug didn't bother to open them again until the song ended. Even then, he had to force himself to look their way.

TJ was looking at him when he did, the question written in his eyes. They knew each other well. Too well. That closeness meant they could speak with expressions as well as words.

TJ wanted to know if Doug was okay with the dance.

He gave TJ a quick nod and smile and watched his friend visibly relax.

"So...what, um, happens after, you know..." Rosalia looked from TJ to Doug, and he could see her struggling to ask something.

"What happens after the dance?" TJ finished for her.

TJ hadn't released her yet, his hands on her waist, Rosalia's on his forearms. Doug tried to decide if she was holding TJ at bay or keeping him close.

She nodded slowly. "Yeah."

"We kiss our dates good night."

TJ was a man of action. He tipped Rosalia's face up with a finger under her chin. He held her gaze for the count of three, giving her a chance to step away.

Rosalia didn't move back. Instead, she shifted forward.

TJ pressed his lips to hers in a kiss that was seventy-million light years away from friendly. His hands cupped her cheeks as he deepened the kiss, pressing her lips open, and Doug caught a glimpse of their tongues touching.

Doug wasn't aware of standing, of walking toward them, but he must have, because one second he was sitting by the fire, and the next he was beside them.

When TJ released her, he took a step back, his eyes dark with hunger. He looked at Doug and tilted his head toward Rosalia. Just one slight motion, but it told Doug he was okay with what came next.

Doug reached out for Rosalia's hand, using his grip to tug her toward him. "I want to kiss my date good night, too."

Rosalia gave him a shy smile.

"You're so beautiful, Rosie." He'd wanted to say that to her forever, but she hadn't been willing to hear it. Not until tonight.

He wasn't sure what the difference was this time. Whether it was TJ's presence or whether it had something to do with whatever was bothering her.

Doug wasn't in the mood to overanalyze it at the moment. He'd waited years for this chance, and he wasn't going to blow it by thinking.

He grinned at the thought, and Rosalia tilted her head, confused by the sudden change in his demeanor.

He didn't give her a chance to ask. Instead, he tucked his arm around her, placing his palm at the small of her back and pulling her flush against him. With his free hand, he ran his fingers through her wavy, thick black hair and kissed her.

He felt like Prince Charming to her Snow White as she mewed softly, her hands wrapping around his neck. Like TJ, he wanted a taste of her sweetness. Their lips parted at the same time and he touched her tongue with his. She was delicious—chocolate and marshmallows with a hint of the hard apple cider she liked to drink.

Doug could kiss her forever. He broke away, intending it to only be a second's reprieve, so they could drink in some much-needed air, but Rosalia released him, taking two steps back before he could resume the kiss.

"Rosie," he whispered. He didn't want it to end here. He needed so much more than just one kiss from her.

She blinked rapidly as she glanced from him to TJ.

"Thank you for the dances," she said. "And the…" Her whispered words faded. "Good night."

Rosalia turned and quickly returned to her RV, leaving him and TJ standing there in her wake.

"TJ—" Doug started, after they'd let a painfully long minute slide by without words.

"No," TJ cut in. "I know you, know you think you have to put words to everything that pops into your head, but we're not talking about this."

Doug didn't argue. In truth, he'd been about to suggest they sleep on what just happened, take some time to wrap their own heads around it before they talked it out. "Okay."

TJ nodded his head good night and headed for their tent.

Doug returned to his chair. The fire was dying down, and he let the flames hypnotize him for a long while.

If only the sparks and embers could burn away the heavy sensation that had just settled over him.

So much for feeling peaceful.

Chapter Four

TJ lay back on the sleeping bag inside the tent. It was late afternoon, and he'd decided to do something he hadn't done since elementary school. Take a nap.

Not that sleep was coming easily.

Or…at all.

He'd been with the research team a month, and he had to say that so far, storm chasing was boring work.

After the downpour the first night, the skies had cleared and September had treated them to nothing but sunshine and cool breezes. If he were at the beach, it would be heaven. But considering their entire purpose was to study severe storms and tornadoes, it wasn't shaping up to be a successful trip.

Regardless, TJ had been grateful for the time to gather his bearings. At least for the first couple of weeks. Doug had given him—covertly—a crash course on the camera equipment, all of which was far superior to the cast-off crap they'd used during high school. They had taken the beginner's lessons away from the campsite at TJ's request because he didn't want the others—mainly Rosalia—to see how little he knew. It wasn't based on the fear she'd let him go. Doug had emphatically reassured him that would never happen.

Nope.

It was based on the same thing that made too many of TJ's decisions in life. Pride. He had too fucking much of it. And even though he knew it wasn't a particularly endearing character trait, he couldn't let it go.

Doug had also spent a few hours each day teaching him the video-editing software. While TJ found the editing concepts fascinating and was glad to learn it, it also drove home exactly how far Doug had surpassed him.

In high school, they'd done the filmmaking together, and TJ had looked forward to those afternoons more than anything in his life. They'd go to Compass Ranch after school and spend hours taking video of the animals, the hands, the land. Once they had mastered the cameras and the editing software, they'd started heading to the football field to get footage of practice or the gymnasium to capture the basketball team.

Because it was just the two of them, and they'd billed themselves as CPSN, they also had to take turns in front of the camera. TJ had assumed Doug would want that role full-time because of his fun-loving, center-of-attention personality.

But that hadn't been the case. Doug had insisted on sharing the spotlight, claiming most newscasts had two anchors. He forced TJ to climb out of his self-imposed shell and talk to people. At the time, TJ had hated it, hated having to make conversation with people when it was a lot easier—and safer—to just blend into the background. He had mastered disappearing up until high school. Hiding bruises from his teachers and friends, skipping school on days when the injuries were too visible, or he didn't feel like he could fake being okay when he wasn't.

Doug always saw the stuff he was hiding. And their junior year, he stopped letting him get away with it. Not in an in-your-face way. That wasn't Doug's style.

Instead, his friend showed him how to be a normal teenager without having to pretend. He invited him over for dinner several times a week so he could spend time with a loving family, agreed to start the journalism club with him so TJ would have a reason to stay out of the house and at school. But more than that, through CPSN, Doug had taken the sullen, quiet boy he'd been in middle school and taught him how to make friends. By senior year, they were two of the most popular guys in their class. Doug had walked away with the Most Likely to Become a Stand-up Comedian superlative, while TJ got the Most Changed Since Sixth Grade nod.

And he knew his peers—even he—considered that change a positive one. Or at least it had been.

When he was with Doug, he was laughing. It was the reason he'd walk through fire for the man. TJ's ability to feel happiness would have most definitely been squashed completely by Thorn if Doug hadn't constantly been around, ready to pick him up with a kind word or crack him up with some joke or prank.

TJ had never seen himself following in his father's footsteps until a couple years ago.

Doug had taken off with the research team for a second spring, and TJ had been left alone for several months. It hadn't dawned on him until Doug returned that he'd regressed back to the boy he'd been in middle school.

Doug had made some dirty joke that had TJ doubled over with laughter, tears streaming down his face. And that was when he realized he hadn't laughed—not even once—in all the time Doug had been gone.

Worse than that, TJ had found himself sitting at the end of Slim's bar alone a few times, drinking a beer under the guise of trying to catch his father coming in after whatever that week's shitty part-time job, to stop him before he started tossing the whiskey back.

As TJ lay there, he was forced to admit it wasn't just his dad that had driven him into the bar. It was his own need to escape the loneliness, the depression, the heaviness that never seemed to leave him.

Unfortunately, that awareness didn't change anything during Doug's last trip. When his friend was away, TJ plodded through the days, the same horrible routine of dreary work followed by mopping his drunk-ass dad off the floor and putting the man to bed as he suffocated TJ in all his hate—of Comptons and gays and basically every other minority on the planet. Then TJ would sit in the living room, wondering if his dad had left enough liquor in the bottle to send him to oblivion as well.

Doug slid the zipper up and stuck his head in the tent. "Still not sleeping?"

TJ shook his head. "Nope. But this might be even better. I'm relaxing."

Doug grinned. "That *is* better. Eric, Justin and I are going to take a walk. Rosie is in her RV doing something that looks really boring."

"Science is hard," TJ said with a chuckle. They'd adopted that line the second day in camp, he and Doug saying it whenever Rosalia forgot who she was talking to and started saying stuff that sounded more like gibberish and Pig Latin than actual words.

Every time they pulled it out, she rolled her eyes, giggled, and then dumbed it down for them. Rosalia was clearly a brilliant scientist, but she never made him or Doug feel stupid for their lack of knowledge about the weather. More than that, she built them up, constantly pointing out their incredible skill with the cameras, while declaring she had "no eye" for the amazing things they filmed. She simply asserted that everyone brought their own unique skills to the table and that was what made them a successful team.

They teased her about pulling the boss card a lot, but TJ was certain she was exactly the type of person he'd love to work for one day.

Whenever that thought crossed his mind, he recalled the job he'd left a month earlier at the lumberyard. Earl, the manager, had cussed him up one side and down the other when he'd called from the road, an hour out of Compton Pass, to quit at the last minute.

TJ had been so focused on packing up and then questioning his sanity as they drove farther and farther away from home, that he'd forgotten all about the fact he'd been scheduled to work that day.

"I'm planning to take some stills of the reservoir. Justin's dropping a line in. Poor bastard is determined to catch a fish."

"Tell him bait might help."

"Last chance to come with us," Doug said.

TJ shook his head. "Happy here. Feeling sort of boneless. Wanna hang on to that for a while."

"See you in bit." Doug waved and zipped the tent back up.

TJ reached for his phone and fired up Rosalia's YouTube channel. Whenever he could manage a few minutes alone, he'd click on her channel, watching her shows with captivated interest.

It didn't take him more than five minutes to figure out there was probably a huge contingency of her followers who were male and watching simply for her. She was fucking gorgeous on screen, but the camera didn't capture a tenth of her true beauty.

The more he got to know her, the more he understood Doug's infatuation.

Hell, the more he *shared* Doug's infatuation.

By tacit agreement, the three of them hadn't discussed the dances or kisses. Not a single word was spoken, but TJ didn't believe for a minute that they weren't all thinking about that night. A lot. God, it was *all* he could think about.

It also didn't slow down the flirting. Doug didn't seem capable of keeping his hands off her, always reaching out to hold her hand or tickle her playfully or ruffle her hair. As for TJ, he found himself feeling things he'd never felt for another woman. Protective. Possessive. He wasn't sure how to batten those things down. He'd spent a lifetime holding everyone at bay. Everyone except Doug...and now, Rosalia.

Coming here had been a mistake. And not just because it meant leaving his dad unchaperoned.

As if that thought summoned a ghost, his phone rang. He recognized the number. It was Slim, at the bar. The poor man had phoned close to a dozen times since TJ left town—and his father no less than twenty—but thus far, TJ had ignored them all, not wanting to take the calls in front of the others.

He'd regretted the few disparaging comments he made about his family lineage to Rosalia the first night he was here, almost instantly. Since then, he'd kept things light, casual, professional. Whenever the subject of his life came up, he deflected the questions and changed the subject. His hesitance to speak about himself hadn't gone unnoticed and the inquiries eventually stopped.

He clicked on his phone. "Hello."

"Thank fucking Jesus. Where the hell have you been, TJ?"

"I'm in Kansas." Rosalia had set them up at a state campground in Milford, claiming it was central to the research area and would make travel quicker and easier whenever a storm hit.

"Kansas? But…well, hell. That makes sense, I guess. When you gettin' back?"

"December." Even as he said it, TJ knew he'd never be able to stay here that long. Thorn would fuck something up and TJ would go back. He hated that about himself, but Thorn was the only family he had, and he'd made a promise to his mother. While the guy was a huge prick and pain in the ass, TJ couldn't shake the sense of responsibility that told him Thorn was his to take care of. It wasn't fair to set him loose on the good people of Compton Pass, so TJ tried to carry the weight alone.

If Doug had shown up on his front door any other day than the one he had, TJ wouldn't have made this journey, not for love nor money. Not even for friendship.

But Doug had caught him at his lowest point yet.

TJ had been sitting in the kitchen alone, staring at a bottle of whiskey and seriously considering downing the thing. He'd never gotten drunk in his life. Not once. He wasn't a teetotaler. It was nothing like that. He had just spent too much time with a mean drunk. TJ was afraid to find out how consuming too much alcohol would affect him. He was terrified of losing control—of his faculties or his temper because of the voice in the back of his head that said once he took that leap, he'd never turn back. So he'd have a glass of wine with dinner or a couple beers by the campfire, just to be social, and that was it.

That day, he was done fighting the inclination, the temptation. He'd wanted to get fucked-up. Wanted to drown every dark, horrible, stinking place inside him with the whiskey, wanted to use it to disappear from his miserable life.

He'd actually had the bottle open and to his lips when Doug knocked on the door. The sound caught him so unaware, he'd dropped it, the bottle shattering loudly on the tile floor.

Something about the shattered glass and strong smell of whiskey pulled him back to his senses.

Then he'd opened the door to Doug. And his invitation.

TJ had agreed to the trip because he didn't want to go back into that kitchen, didn't want to face what he'd almost done, what he was afraid he might still follow through on.

"You can't stay gone until December, TJ," Slim said, pulling him back to the present.

"Actually, I can. I have a job that's going to keep me away."

"What job? What about your dad?"

"Slim—" TJ started.

"He spent a few nights in jail a couple weeks ago. Got shitfaced. When you didn't answer, I called the cops and he took a swing at Sawyer. Didn't the sheriff call you?"

"No. He didn't." But TJ's gut told him Sawyer had probably called Doug. Unlike him, Doug typically spoke to at least one member of his family every day. Not because he was homesick or a mama's boy or anything. It was just because there were so freaking many of them and they were all close.

He wasn't surprised Doug had kept the information to himself, but they'd definitely have a chat about it when his friend got back from the reservoir.

"He's on a bender, man. Worse than usual. Lost his job at the butcher shop and I've banned him from the bar."

TJ didn't say he thought Slim should have done that years ago. He suspected the only reason he hadn't was because he could make some money off Thorn and the second he got unruly, he knew TJ would be there to drag him out.

"Sounds like he won't be your problem anymore then."

Slim sighed. "Rumor has it he's been driving himself over to that biker bar in Clarke."

TJ rubbed his eyes wearily and pulled himself to a sitting position on the sleeping bag. So much for boneless. The tightness in his shoulders reappeared with a vengeance.

His dad had lost his driver's license six months earlier, something that probably would have happened sooner if TJ wasn't always picking him up at Slim's after work every time he slipped his leash. That night, the battery on his phone had died and he hadn't realized, hadn't gotten the call. Like a dumbass, he'd actually hoped it meant his dad had gone straight home from work.

"I'll give Sawyer a call. Tell him to be on the lookout." TJ would never forgive himself if his dad hurt someone else on the road while driving drunk. "Maybe he can impound his car or something."

"Yeah," Slim didn't sound convinced. "Maybe. You sure you can't get back earlier?"

"I'm sure," TJ lied.

"Okay, well, I'll stop bothering you then."

They said their goodbyes, and TJ sat staring at the inside of the tent.

Rosalia had made a comment last night, wondering how they could stand to sleep on the ground night after night. TJ hadn't mentioned that he was used to sleeping rough. His bedroom at home consisted of a shitty mattress on the floor and a beat-up dresser. At some point in his life, they'd had decent furniture, but TJ had sold off most of it piece by piece over the years to bail his dad out of jail or to pay legal fees for his drunk-in-public and drunk-driving charges.

He tried to tell himself it was time to go home. Time to stop being selfish and get back to reality. His dad hadn't been able to hold down a job for more than a few weeks in years, which meant the little money his dad had made at the butcher shop was probably long gone.

TJ had signed his last paycheck from the lumberyard and left it on the kitchen table when he headed out with Doug. In the back of his mind, he had figured he would be back in Compton Pass before his dad blew through the few measly hundred bucks.

But that was a month ago. October had arrived, and there was no way his dad had any money left. For booze or food. TJ had sent the first small check from this gig straight to the bank to pay the mortgage, then he'd called Doug's brother, James, and asked him to check in on his dad. James promised he would, said he'd take over some groceries even, but TJ couldn't keep asking the Comptons to step in. It was his responsibility. His promise.

So yeah. It was time to go home.

He looked at his phone, considered doing a search for a bus station nearby.

Instead, he clicked back onto YouTube and continued playing Rosalia's show.

He didn't want to leave.

In his entire life, TJ had never done a goddamn thing for himself. This trip, this time with Doug and Rosalia, was for him.

If he went back home now, it wouldn't be long before he was back at that kitchen table again, staring at the bottle.

"Hey."

He glanced up to see Rosalia peering through the open mesh.

"Thought I heard," she paused, grinning, "my voice over here."

He stood up, unzipped the tent and joined her outside. "Doug assigned me homework," he lied. "Wants me to study the camera angles he's been using in your videos."

"Oh. That's cool." She blushed lightly, her common reaction to him, and he was hard-pressed not to reach over and run his knuckles along her cheek. He wondered if the pretty pink was warm to the touch. "Should I ask what you think of...me in the show?"

"Seriously? You're a rock star, Rosalia. Beautiful, intelligent. You make me want to go back to school to study meteorology. If only—"

"Science wasn't hard," she added, finishing his joke.

"Exactly."

"Are you okay? You looked...deep in thought when I first walked over."

He wondered how long she'd been standing there.

"I'm fine." He gestured toward the camp chairs. Doug had started a fire at lunchtime, declaring hot dogs were only edible when they were burned black. No one had disagreed with that assessment.

TJ threw another log on the fire, while Rosalia opened the cooler. "Want a soda? Bottle of water? Beer?"

He was seriously tempted by the beer but shoved the feeling away. "Water's cool. Thanks," he said as she handed it to him and the two of them sat down. This was the first time he'd ever been completely alone with Rosalia. Doug had remarked a few days ago that he was worried about her, claiming she was quieter than normal. Since TJ had nothing to compare her current behavior to, he didn't feel the same sense of unease. To him, she seemed sweet and sort of shy and...fuck...just his type.

"You didn't feel like joining the others at the lake?" she asked.

"No. Doug assures me that all this downtime won't last, so I thought I'd take advantage of it."

Rosalia nodded. "I'm sure it must seem very dull right now. Storm chasing always looks so exciting on the TV shows, but in reality...it's more often us setting off weather balloons in church parking lots—"

"Church lots?"

She laughed. "There are a ton of church lots, especially in the South. And six days of the week, they're vacant. We try to get ahead of the storms usually."

"What happens after you send the balloon up?"

"We find a gas station, eat boiled peanuts and wait for it to feed us data."

"Wow," he said, purposely adopting a bored tone.

"Right? Actually, the GPS system on the balloons feeds us the data in near real time as it ascends." She spent a few minutes explaining how the balloons worked and how they could interpret the data it provided. TJ tried to pay attention to her words, but he was too distracted by the way her long dark hair was laying over her shoulders and the way her brown eyes looked almost black in this light. She was beauty incarnate.

TJ took a long chug from the bottle of water and forced himself to concentrate.

"...to capture how the temperature, moisture, and wind are changing."

He nodded, hoping to hide the fact he'd missed too much of her lesson. "I've been watching your videos. In one, the tornado seemed really close."

"I'd never put myself or the team in danger, if that's what you're worried about. We stay well out of the path. I know the video you're talking about. It was Doug's fancy camerawork that made it look a lot more impressive than it was. That tornado was actually dying out and nearly half a mile away. And while tornadoes can happen at any time, we're not in peak season right now, so I suspect this trip will consist more of severe storms than twisters."

Half a mile didn't seem all that far away to him, but he kept that thought to himself. "I wasn't worried about the danger to me."

"Oh, I wasn't implying..." Rosalia gave him an adorable little shrug that proved she *had* thought that.

"You have a cool job," he said. "You've really found your calling."

Rosalia's blush deepened. "Seems like you have you too." Like him, she didn't seem to enjoy being the center of any conversation.

He wouldn't call driving a forklift around and moving wood all day a cool job, and it sure as fuck wasn't calling to him as a dream job.

"I mean...if you're anything like Doug. He's mad about filming and editing our shows," she added, and he realized she wasn't talking about the lumberyard. He thought of how it felt to work with a video camera again after so many years away from his passion. Like Doug, he loved filming, loved trying to capture the essence of a place, the excitement of a moment or the unmasked expression of a person. "There's nothing like holding a camera." He started to add *again* but stopped himself just in time.

"Did you and Doug go to college together?"

Her question took him aback. Apparently, Doug had respected his wishes, hadn't outted him as a complete novice. "No."

She waited for him to say more. She always waited. For a month solid, she'd opened the door for him to share, and he'd slammed it right back in her face time after time.

Unfortunately, the phone call from Slim had put him in a bad place, reminded him of how tired he was of TJ Nicholas's life. He wanted to be someone like Rosalia. Like Doug. They'd taken their dreams and created happy, productive lives for themselves.

TJ had pissed away the years since graduation. Just once, he wanted to be someone who'd done something more than take care of an alcoholic father and drive a forklift. But the truth was, that was all he knew. Staying away didn't change that, didn't make him a different person or a better one.

He searched for a way to break the silence. Rosalia toyed with the locket she always wore. TJ pointed to it. "Who gave you the locket?"

She smiled. "My grandmother. It was hers, a gift from my grandfather on their wedding day. She gave it to me the day I got my doctorate."

"It's pretty."

Rosalia looked down at it, and he thought for a second he saw the beginning of tears in her eyes. "Grandma said Granddad would have been very proud of his granddaughter, the doctor. She said that by wearing the locket, I'd always be able to carry a piece of them, of their love, with me."

TJ wished he had something from his mother that he carried around like that. It had never occurred to him until that minute he didn't have anything of hers with him. Not that there was much left. And what did remain was at home...with Thorn. He should have packed something. He could use a little of her love right now.

All he had with him was a tattered, faded picture of his mom that he carried in his wallet. "That was sweet of your grandma. Where's your grandfather now?"

Suddenly, he understood her tears.

"He died. He was killed by a drunk driver when I was six. I know that seems too young to have very many memories, but I remember him so well. And..." Her voice broke. "I remember the night the police knocked on the door to tell us the news. My grandmother was waiting for him to pick her up. She and my mother had spent the day together, baking for the holidays. I'd just snuck out of the kitchen with a fresh-baked sugar cookie. It was tree-shaped with green and red sprinkles. No one knew I was there when they opened the door. The policeman said something I couldn't hear and my grandma fell to the floor. She just crumpled. My mother bent down with her, wrapped her arms around her, and they fell apart together. It was the first time I'd ever seen either of them cry."

She shook herself from her painful memory, wiping her eyes. "Sorry," she said with a rueful grin. "I have no idea why I just told you all that."

TJ swallowed heavily. A guilt he didn't want to feel gripped him as he recalled Slim's words. Thorn had been in jail. He was driving drunk, endangering others. How could he let his father rip apart a family the way Rosalia's had been?

If he was going home, it had to be now. The longer he stayed, the harder it would be to leave. To walk away from Rosalia, who was stealing more and more of his heart each day. To leave Doug behind.

Stay or go.

Stay or...

"Rosalia," he started, the answer clear to him.

"Hey, Rosie!" Eric yelled, hustling toward them, Doug and Justin a few feet behind. "Was checking the weather forecasts on my phone and there's a big-ass storm gathering near the Kansas/Oklahoma border. Has some serious twister potential."

Rosalia was up and out of her seat. "Let's break camp and try to beat it."

The next thirty minutes were a whirlwind of activity as the tents and the pop-up camper were taken down, their equipment, coolers and chairs all thrown into the vehicles. TJ couldn't believe how quickly they were able to pack and get on the road.

Eric and Justin took the lead position, Eric serving as navigator. Rosalia was behind them in her RV as he and Doug brought up the rear in Doug's truck.

Doug was grinning ear to ear, clearly in his element. "Here's where it gets exciting."

The trip took them nearly four hours, the sky growing darker the closer they got to their destination of Stillwater, Oklahoma.

71

They traveled down a country lane, the area sparsely populated, mercifully. Eric actually found a Baptist church in the middle of nowhere—Rosalia hadn't been joking about the abundance of churches—and guided them to the empty lot.

They hopped out of their vehicles, all of them convening in Rosalia's RV.

"Wind's pretty high. You still plan to set a balloon off?" Justin asked. "We'd have to be generous with the helium to make sure it goes straight up and not into one of those trees over there."

Rosalia sat down and clicked a few buttons on her laptop.

Doug looked at TJ and murmured, "She's checking the radar."

Rosalia looked up. "I don't think we'd garner any useful information if we set it off now. Our primary goal is the pre-storm environment, how the moisture, instability, and wind shear are evolving. We're too late to grab that data. This is a full-blown storm."

Doug glanced out the window. "It's a hell of a storm, strong wind, thunder, heavy rain. Any funnel clouds forming, Eric?"

Eric was looking at his own laptop and he shook his head. "Not yet, but that doesn't mean they *won't* form. All the conditions are right."

Doug rubbed his chin. "Been a pretty uneventful fall. I feel like we should take advantage of this. Why don't we capture some footage right now? If nothing evolves, we can use it for B-roll in future shows."

Rosalia seemed to like that idea. "Okay. Let's do it. This is a great storm to use to discuss supercells. I've had a couple high school teachers email to request a show about them."

"We're taking requests now?" Justin asked. "What are we? The radio?"

Meanwhile, TJ gave her a blank stare that must have amused her, so she tried to explain her plan for the show. "Thunderstorms begin with pockets of rising air called cells. Large and energetic cells rise more quickly, and we call them supercells."

"Save it for the camera," Doug said, his case open as he started putting it together.

She laughed. "Let me just grab some rain gear. I'm going to get so wet."

"That's what she said," Doug joked.

Rosalia laughed lightly, but her suddenly pink cheeks betrayed her. She'd obviously played out that fantasy before. TJ wondered who was with her though—him or Doug?

Or both of them?

Doug spotted her reaction, too, and his expression sobered. Great. Now all three of them were thinking about sex.

TJ would bet his last dollar neither Doug nor Rosalia were playing it out the way he was.

Justin and Eric, mercifully, had sprung into action the moment Rosalia said they were going outside, so they missed the entire exchange.

"I can set up a live feed," Justin said. "We've been talking about that, and this seems like a great place to give it a try."

Doug readily agreed, as he and Justin had worked out all the particulars for a live broadcast over the past two weeks and they were chomping at the bit to do one.

Rosalia was less enthusiastic. "No room for mistakes when you go live feed."

Doug was ready to counter that argument with the compromise they'd come up with. "Let's do the trial run Justin suggested. We just send the link to his classmates at the university for this first attempt."

Rosalia shook her head at Justin's and Doug's puppy-dog expressions. "I hate when you guys gang up on me with cuteness. Fine. Okay."

For the next few minutes, they gathered their equipment and put on their rain gear.

TJ nearly lost his footing as he stepped out of the RV, the wind catching him off guard, packing a serious punch.

Doug grabbed his upper arm, steadying him. "I got you."

"Thanks, man. Wasn't expecting such strong wind." TJ swallowed heavily when Doug released him. There was too much shit swimming around in his head right now. Between Slim's call, his deepening feelings for Rosalia and his overactive sexual fantasies, he was hard-pressed to concentrate on the task at hand. Which was bad, because the storm was raging and it was taking all the strength he had just to keep a firm grip on the camera.

Rosalia was obviously more accustomed to strong wind because, despite her petite size, she was doing a better job combating the gale force pushing against her back.

She wore a large-brimmed hat that kept precious little of the rain out of her eyes. She held a weatherproof microphone as she led him and Doug away from the RV. The church had built a picnic shelter near a playground, so they stepped under the roof briefly to get a bearing on their surroundings. He could see she and Doug both looking for the perfect spot to broadcast from.

"What's wrong with doing it under here?" TJ asked.

"Oh, we'll do a lot of it under here, but we need an opening scene."

TJ recalled that every single episode of *Light as Air* began with Rosalia out in the elements, speaking to the camera as she was pummeled by wind, rain, sometimes even hail.

Doug looked around. "We don't need to go far. I can set up the shot to capture the horizon." He looked at TJ. "We just have to be careful not to pan out too far. Don't want to get the church or the playground in the scene. Once we've got the opening footage, we can walk back here and Rosie can do the majority of her lesson on supercells under the shelter. Luckily, there are no trees too close to hit us if they fall."

She studied the area and pointed. "That one possibly could, but that's not my main concern. We need to work fast, in case of lightning or funnel clouds forming."

TJ hated the whole conversation, suddenly worried about the tree, the potential tornado *and* the lightning. His protector instincts roared to the surface, and he was tempted to suggest they forget the whole idea of an opening scene and just film the footage under the shelter. Or in the RV. Or better yet, can the entire show.

Instead, against every fiber of his being telling him to get Doug and Rosalia inside to safety, he followed them about fifty yards from the shelter, fighting to breathe as the wind slammed into him, straight on. Somehow he found the strength to lift the camera. Studying Doug's location in front of Rosalia, he picked a spot that would work as secondary footage, capturing her slightly from the right, while keeping the church and playground out of the frame and maintaining the unhindered backdrop.

Justin and Eric were inside the RV. Eric would make the camera cuts for the live feed. In the meantime, they would capture everything on the cameras' hard drives to download later for the YouTube version of the show.

They'd only just started when a bolt of lightning struck a different tree a few hundred yards away. A large branch splintered and fell to the ground. It sounded like a bomb had been dropped on their heads.

TJ lowered the camera, shocked when Doug gave him a quick shake of the head, he and Rosalia still recording. She was actually excited about the lightning flash and making some comment about how lucky they were to capture that on film.

Then Eric yelled at them from the door of the RV. "We've got funnel clouds forming to the west. Hurry up and record this bit and we'll move closer!"

TJ looked that direction and spotted what Eric had seen on the horizon. Logically, he could see the tornado wasn't particularly large and it was a fair distance away. Neither of those facts calmed him down. He'd never seen a tornado in his life and he really didn't fucking like it.

"Third," Doug yelled. "Start filming again. You're missing it."

TJ didn't pick his camera back up.

"Are you crazy?" He had to speak loudly to be heard over the howling wind and rumble of thunder.

Rosalia had been studying the funnel cloud, waiting for TJ to resume taping. She was clearly surprised by his outburst.

Doug narrowed his eyes. "What are you doing, TJ?"

"This is insane. She's in danger out here."

"What?" Rosalia asked.

"Am I the only person who saw that lightning strike the tree? Who sees that goddamn tornado? Get *closer*? Did he seriously say we're moving closer to that?" TJ gestured toward the huge branch on the ground before waving his hand toward the west. "If that branch had hit anyone, it wouldn't have just injured them. It would have killed them." He looked at Rosalia. "It would have killed you."

"It wasn't anywhere near us." Rosalia looked over her shoulder, dismissing the broken tree as if it were nothing. "Can we start again? We really should do this fast. Because, you know," she said with a laugh as she pointed up, "lightning." And then toward the twister, "Tornado."

TJ's sudden anger grew hotter at her continued nonchalant attitude. "Get back to the shelter, Rosalia. Or better yet, get in the RV."

"What? Why are you acting like this? You realize we tape these shows in severe weather, right? What did you think this was going to be like?"

Doug raised his free hand, waving it in surrender. "Let's all take a breather, okay? It's TJ's first time out, Rosie. It took me some time to get used to the tornadoes, too."

Rosalia's hands were on her hips, her eyes shooting sparks. "That doesn't give him the right to boss me around. This is my—"

"I'm not getting used to this," TJ interrupted. "You're putting yourself in danger. Both of you. What's wrong with you, Doug? You say you care about her," TJ said, turning on his friend. "But you can't tell me you'd let your mother or sister or female cousins do this without dragging their asses back inside."

"Excuse me," Rosalia yelled. "But who the hell do you think you are? I don't need men protecting me. I'm completely capable of taking care of—" Her voice broke unexpectedly, and TJ realized she was on the verge of tears. "Never mind. We're obviously done here."

Justin popped his head out of the RV and yelled across the parking lot to them. "Uh, you guys remember this is a live feed, right?"

Doug quickly hit the pause button on his camera. "Fuck."

"You aired all of that?" Rosalia asked, horrified.

Justin jogged out to them, wearing nothing more than a T-shirt and jeans, both of which were soaked through by the time he reached them. "Sorry about that, Rosie. I was watching the action between you three, forgot about the live feed."

"Can we have this conversation inside?" TJ persisted.

"Eric said the funnel cloud dissipated. Tornado is a dud. And the storm is already starting to die out."

TJ didn't give a shit, even as he looked over his shoulder to confirm the twister had vanished.

Justin, ever the joker, had shitty timing when he said, "So, my friends were texting me during all that. They want to know which cameraman you're dating."

"No more live feeds," Rosalia muttered as she stalked back to the shelter. "Ever."

"Man. I think that would be a loss," Justin said, grinning widely as they all followed her. "There was some pretty serious sexual tension out here. I'm surprised the sparks you three are setting off didn't create even more lightning."

Rosalia dropped down onto the picnic table. "Go away, Justin."

He looked around, aware that he'd interrupted them mid-fight—and none of them were ready to laugh about what had happened. "Oh. Yeah. Hey, listen, since we're done here, you mind if me and Eric split?"

"Split?" Rosalia asked. She sounded tired all of a sudden.

"Eric's got a girl he's sweet on who lives about forty miles away. You okay if we head there for the night? She promised us a hot home-cooked dinner and, while Eric's getting to sleep in a real bed, I'm cool with the couch since it includes chicken parm."

Rosalia nodded. "That sounds great. The two of you go on. We'll reconvene tomorrow."

If TJ weren't still so enraged, he might have felt bad for Rosalia's subdued tone. She'd been energized when they'd stepped out of the RV. That excitement was definitely gone now.

Then the sky lit up with another flash of lightning and a loud crash of thunder, despite Justin's assertion that the storm was dying.

Fuck this.

His temper spiked and shot his blood pressure into orbit again.

He couldn't land. Not on this. This was insane.

Chapter Five

None of them spoke as they watched Eric and Justin climb into their car and pull out of the parking lot.

Even when the three of them were completely alone again, Doug wasn't sure how to break the silence. Primarily because he agreed with both of them.

Like TJ, he hated seeing Rosalia in danger, and while he'd been with the team long enough to appreciate the precautions and care she took, the only way he'd managed to accept things was to stay as close to her as possible.

But Rosalia was right, too. This was her job. More than that, this was her passion. She was smart and careful, but driven. Watching her talk about weather, about these storms, had actually become a bit of a turn-on for him. Because she was so animated and excited, he couldn't help but get wrapped up in her enthusiasm. She made him want to be a part of it.

Rosalia shivered, wrapping her arms around her middle, and suddenly Doug knew exactly what to say. Even in the shelter, they were getting wet, the wind sending enough of the deluge pounding down around them under the roof to drench them even more.

Walking over, he sat down next to her, taking her hand in his. "Why don't you head back to the RV? Change into some dry clothes. TJ and I will give you a few minutes, then we'll join you inside. Okay?"

She nodded, then stood slowly. He noticed she didn't spare TJ a single glance as she walked by him.

TJ was leaning against a corner post, arms crossed, scowl firmly in place.

"That went well."

Doug's joke succeeded...a little. While TJ didn't crack a smile, the tension in his shoulders gave way and his arms dropped.

"I don't think I can do this job. I'm going back to Compton Pass."

Doug thought about that, trying to decide if TJ's words were sincere or knee-jerk. "Does this have anything to do with Slim's phone call earlier?"

TJ had blindsided him about two hours into their mad dash to the storm, asking him if he knew about his dad taking a swing at Sawyer.

While it had been easy to fib through omission, it was impossible for Doug to lie to his friend's face, so he'd confessed to knowing about his dad's stint in jail. He had expected TJ to be pissed off about it, but instead, he'd merely nodded and let the subject drop.

That should have been a big warning sign, but Doug had misread it, interpreted it as TJ turning a corner on his past, moving on.

"This doesn't have anything to do with my father," TJ replied, his voice suddenly as tired as Rosalia's had been.

Given TJ's heated response to Rosalia and the storm, Doug knew exactly what reaction his next words would generate. He said them anyway. "I think this has everything to do with Thorn."

TJ's scowl deepened, his rage resurfacing, hotter than before. "Don't pull that crap on me."

"What crap?"

"You can't crawl around inside my head and tell me how I think, how I feel, Doug. Not everything in my world revolves around Thorn."

Doug disagreed, but he was smart enough to keep his mouth shut about it. "Fine. So why don't you tell me why you can't do the job?"

TJ fell silent. It was all the answer Doug needed.

"It's Rosie, isn't it? You want her."

TJ shook his head too quickly, a dead giveaway that Doug had hit the nail on the head.

"No, man. I know how you feel about her. I've only known her a month."

"I've known you since you were five, Third. You're the king of love at first sight. I saw it with Beth Kincaid in second grade when she gave you the big Valentine's card and a lollipop, while the rest of us sad saps just got the standard card and a sticker."

TJ chuckled. "Beth was hot in those flannel shirts and leggings."

Doug rolled his eyes, but didn't disagree. "Every boy in class had a crush on her. She picked you."

"Hardly think you can make a blanket statement about me rushing to fall in love based on a second-grade romance."

"Maybe not, but I saw it again the first night we were here, sitting in Rosie's RV when she shared her lasagna with us." What Doug didn't say was, he hadn't seen it any of the years between TJ's mom dying and now.

"It doesn't matter."

"Why not?"

"You were there first."

Doug snorted. "This isn't finders keepers, TJ."

"She doesn't mix work and play. You said so yourself."

Doug sighed. "I think she might break that rule for you."

TJ smirked miserably. "I'm not the only one she'd break it for."

If TJ had said that last spring, Doug would have flat-out denied it, but he'd spent the last two weeks reliving that dance by the campfire over and over. Regardless, he dismissed the comment, unwilling to let TJ get away with changing the subject. "I don't think she was as offended by your alpha-male, caveman-style tactics out there in that storm as she pretended."

"Not sure where you got that impression. Woman looked plenty pissed off to me. Besides, there's a difference between attraction and affection."

Doug frowned. "What's that mean?"

"We're attracted to each other."

"Attraction can turn to more. Can turn into affection," Doug said quietly.

"You're right. And you're miles ahead of me on both. I know you don't believe me, but Rosalia does have feelings for you. How many times has she made that work husband joke? And whenever she chooses a seat, it's the one next to you. I gotta admit it. I know we're best friends, man, and I know that's rock solid, but when I watch the two of you, I feel a little jealous how tight you are. The two of you get each other."

Doug closed his eyes, rubbing his forehead wearily. When he opened them again, he rested his elbows on his knees and studied the concrete floor of the shelter. "You and I get each other, too. So I'm just going to say what I'm thinking, because I know you won't judge me or freak out."

"You gonna look at me when you say it?"

Doug lifted his head. "We need to talk to Rosie."

TJ sighed. "If you're telling me I need to apologize, I know that. But that's not going to change the way I feel about her work. It's one thing to watch her sitting at a computer, analyzing data. It's not in me to stand aside while she steps out into the path of these damn storms. I'm not made that way."

"I'm not telling you to apologize."

TJ frowned.

"Well, I mean you should, but that's not what our conversation is going to be about."

"Oookay," TJ drawled. "So what are we saying?"

"We're gonna ask her to invite us to her bed."

TJ stared at him without speaking. The lack of shock on his face told Doug his friend had come to the same conclusion.

"But you already knew that, didn't you?" Doug asked.

TJ still leaned against the post. The storm had subsided, the sky dropping nothing more than a steady rain instead of the torrential downpour earlier. The wind was still whipping around, but it came in occasional gusts now.

"And how do you think that's going to go down after what just happened between her and me?" TJ had a point. Not a valid one, but a point.

Because Doug had a pretty damn good idea how it was going down. Actually, how *they* were going down.

"Let's go find out."

TJ pushed off the post. "Okay."

He chuckled at Doug's surprised expression when he said, "That was easier than I expected."

"I've been with Rosalia for a month solid. Spent the last two weeks trying not to think about that kiss by the campfire. Figured you wouldn't like it if I jerked off every night in the sleeping bag next to you."

Doug would have laughed if he hadn't been battling the same affliction. "I hear you, man."

"Worst-case scenario?" TJ asked as they started walking toward the RV.

Doug nodded. It was a game they'd started playing after catching Doug's mom in the living room, crying over an episode of *This is Us*. They'd been concerned something really bad had happened until they realized the show had provoked the tears. After they teased her for crying so hard over something that wasn't even real, they got sucked into the damn show.

Two of the characters always played Worst-Case Scenario, where they said all their fears out loud, and since then, he and Doug had played it a few times as a joke. This time, it felt a little too real.

"She turns us both down," Doug said.

"She just turns me down."

Doug swallowed heavily. "Or me. Then she fires both of us on the spot."

TJ was quiet for a moment as they let that soak in. "Or she suggests an orgy and insists on including Justin and Eric, too. I sincerely hope to never see Eric's scrawny ass naked."

Doug feigned a shiver, then laughed. "That would be really bad."

"The worst."

They paused just outside the door.

"You sure?" TJ asked.

Doug nodded. There were a million things he didn't have a clue about, but this wasn't one of them. This felt right.

He reached for the knob, but TJ put his hand on his shoulder. "If this goes the way we hope, you're gonna have to stop calling me Third."

Doug laughed. Now that they'd said the worst out loud, Doug figured there wasn't anything they couldn't handle.

TJ knocked on the door. They waited for an invitation, but when it didn't come, their alarm got the better of them and they walked in.

Rosalia wasn't in the front part of the RV, so they shed all their wet rain gear, then made their way down the short corridor to her bedroom.

She was sitting cross-legged on the bed, propped up by pillows and the wall at her back. She was dressed in an old college T-shirt and fleece pants. Her hair was wet from the rain, but combed.

Doug had worried they'd find her crying, but instead, she looked nervous.

Rosalia gestured to her outfit. "My sexiest pajamas."

He tried to make sense of that comment. Was she making fun of her pj's, or had she been aiming for sexy?

"You'd look hot in a burlap sack." TJ was leaning against the doorframe, his alpha male resurfacing.

Doug gave him a pointed glance, waiting for TJ to get the apology out of the way. His contrary friend didn't take him up on the offer.

Instead, he gestured toward the spot next to Rosalia. "You got room for us in there?"

Rosalia licked her lips as she nodded.

TJ claimed her left, sitting next to her on the mattress, his back against the same wall as her. Doug forgot to move until they both looked at him.

Rather than sit directly next to her, he dropped onto the opposite side of the bed from TJ, facing them.

TJ reached down and took her hand, lifting it to his lips. Rosalia watched him, and Doug sensed she was barely breathing.

"Rosie," Doug started. "About earlier—"

She shook her head, stopping him, her gaze still locked on where TJ was kissing her knuckles. She gasped softly when he took one of her fingers into his mouth.

TJ gave her a guilty grin, slowly pulling her finger out until it was freed with a soft pop. "I'm sorry, Rosalia."

She lifted her shoulders casually and gave him a smile that said all was forgiven. Just like that.

"You know why we're here?" TJ asked.

She nodded.

"You okay with that?"

Rosalia's response came slower, but when it did, she nodded again.

"You forget how to talk?"

She narrowed her eyes at TJ's smart-ass question, and Doug was grateful to see her spunkiness return.

"No. But I'm not sure the two of you will like what I have to say."

Doug frowned and scooted closer, reaching out to rest his hand on her knee. He needed to touch her, to show her how much he wanted her. "Say it anyway," he urged.

"The other night…when we were alone by the campfire…"

He nodded to indicate he knew which night she was talking about. It was the only thing he'd been able to think of since.

Rosalia kept her gaze glued on his face. Apparently, she felt safer making this confession to him.

"That was the first night I'd ever been kissed."

Doug tried to make some sense of those words, but it was taking him a minute.

TJ cupped her cheek, turning her to face him. "First kiss?"

She nodded, her face flaming red. "In case you haven't figured it out, I was a nerd in high school. Frizzy hair, thick glasses, no makeup, nose always in a science book. I was the whole package when it comes to teenage nightmares. And it didn't really get better in college. I lived in the science lab with guys just as nerdy as me. We were a whole department of awkward and shy."

"There was no one?" Doug asked, still struggling to catch up.

"I suppose there was one guy in college. He actually used the line 'if there was no gravity on the planet, I'd still fall for you.' I laughed because I thought it was a joke. He admitted to me at his wedding that he'd been seriously in love with me back then, but I never realized. And he didn't have the courage to try after...well...after I laughed. Which I still feel terrible about."

Doug couldn't help it. He laughed. Not at her, but, God, the whole situation. He and TJ had walked into this RV hoping to convince her to join them in a threesome, which was a shocking enough proposal on its own.

Toss in the fact they'd found the only twenty-seven-year-old virgin in the country, and it got a whole lot crazier. How could they expect her to say yes to what they were asking? It was an extreme concept for most woman who *had* sexual experience.

"Worst-case scenario?" Doug murmured, thinking it would make TJ laugh, but his friend wasn't seeing the humor in any of this.

TJ shook his head. "Best case. She's ours. Just ours."

Chapter Six

Rosalia let TJ's words soak in. She had spent every minute since returning to the RV fighting to still her trembling hands. She'd been pissed off at TJ's over-the-top alpha-male behavior during the taping, but in truth, every word had sent tingles straight to her vagina.

By the time she'd reached the shelter, she had been in serious hormone overload, her insides quivery with need.

When Doug leaned close, telling her to change her clothes, that they would come to her, she'd nearly melted into a pile of goo. Somehow, she had found the strength to get to the RV.

That was when she realized she didn't own one single sexy nightie. Or bra and panties set.

She was the world's worst when it came to sex appeal.

So she'd put on the T-shirt and fleece pants and written off the whole crazy idea. There was no way two hotter-than-the-surface-of-the-sun, rugged, gorgeous cowboys would want her, the nerd with granny panties and one ovary.

"Why now?" Doug asked.

She understood his question. For three spring trips, she'd rebuffed his advances. The workaholic professional had actually been proud of that fortitude, that power of resistance.

Then the doctor found the tumor, and she was left with nothing but regret.

"I had surgery in May."

Doug reared back, and she realized her words had come out of left field.

Raising her hands, she hastened to add, "I'm fine. It was a tumor."

His brows creased with genuine alarm. "What? What the hell—"

She was fucking this up. "Benign. It was benign. But they had to take out one of my ovaries."

"Rosie." Doug said her name in a gush of air. "I'm sorry. Why didn't you tell me?"

She lifted one shoulder. "I found out about it a week or two after Jake died. I didn't want to put that on your shoulders."

"That was the wrong thing to do. You had to know I'd want to be there for you."

"I know. But when it turned out to be nothing, I figured everything would go back to normal." She reached out to take both of his hands in hers. "I can't do *that* normal anymore."

"But you're sure you can do this one?" He gave her a comforting smile. "Because there are a lot of folks who wouldn't call this normal at all."

She wasn't sure how to explain it to them in a way they'd understand. Probably because she didn't even know if *she* got it. It had been easy for her to remain a virgin, to never reach for that first kiss, because she'd never been tempted, never met the man who could claim her heart.

Doug had stolen it the first spring he'd joined the team, but she'd resisted his advances for all the wrong reasons.

He made her laugh, made her happy.

She loved him. It was as simple as that.

TJ was something else altogether. He touched somewhere a little more exciting and a lot more forbidden. She wanted him physically. There was no question about that. But there was more to it. She kept coming back to those sad eyes. Something told her they *needed* each other just as much as they wanted each other. The old Rosalia would have backed away from that, thrown the chance away and then regretted it.

She wasn't doing that tonight.

"Does it feel normal to you?" she asked.

Doug nodded. "Yeah. It does."

Rosalia glanced over her shoulder, asking TJ the same question without repeating the words.

TJ pushed her hair over her shoulders, his fingertips grazing her cheek. "We'll take it slow."

She shivered, the response triggered by arousal, not fear. "Not too slow, I hope."

Her flirty words fired a starting pistol. TJ took them to heart. One second, she was completely covered. The next, her T-shirt was tossed over his shoulder, leaving her naked from the waist up.

Given her lack of pretty underwear, she'd opted for wearing none. That seemed bold when she was ninety-nine percent sure nothing would happen.

Now...

She quickly covered herself, cursing the hot flames she could feel erupting in her cheeks. She hated how easily she blushed, always feeling like a silly schoolgirl.

TJ wrapped his large hands around hers, tugging them away.

"You don't have to hide from us, Rosalia." TJ's eyes drifted lower, looking at her breasts. Doug shifted until he was sitting directly behind her. She jerked when his hands reached around to cup them.

"Shoot. Sorry, Rosie. Are my hands cold?"

"No. It's not that." Her heart beat so hard and so fast, she wondered if they could hear it.

"You're shaking," Doug whispered, his lips at her ear.

"I'm not scared." Her words came out too quickly, too loudly.

TJ chuckled. "No one thought you were. For God's sake, you chase tornadoes, darlin'."

Oh damn. A term of endearment.

It no doubt spoke to her innocence that she fell head over heels for TJ in that moment. Maybe she'd pay for that somewhere down the road, but for tonight, she was going with it.

"What do you say we get the talking out of the way now?"

She tilted her head, confused by TJ's suggestion. "I thought we already said it all."

He shook his head. "We covered the tough stuff, rode out the storm. Now we analyze the data. See what we have to work with."

She laughed as TJ started speaking her language. "Wow. Maybe science isn't that hard after all."

Doug snorted behind her. "Jesus, Third."

TJ shot Doug a dirty look. "What did I say about that?"

"Sort of puts a fun spin on that nickname, doesn't it?" she joked.

She and Doug laughed, while TJ gave them a narrow-eyed glare that didn't fool anyone. He was just as amused by it as they were.

"You finished?" TJ asked, the corners of his lips tipped up.

Rosalia giggled. "Yes...Third."

He reached out and pinched one of her nipples, the sharp squeeze catching her by surprise, a weird combination of ouch and wow rumbling through her.

She squeaked.

"That's a cute sound," TJ said. "I'm going to make sure I hear it a few more times tonight."

"Okay," Rosalia replied, more breath than word.

"I know you're a virgin, but are you on the Pill?"

Suddenly, she understood TJ's need for data.

She nodded. "I started taking them after the surgery."

"Toys?"

She frowned. "What?"

"Do you play with toys? Vibrators? Dildos?"

The volcano erupted, painting her cheeks red again as she shook her head. She wondered if her response would change things. She'd grown up in a small house with six brothers, her parents and her grandmother. Privacy was a privilege she got precious little of.

In college, she'd opted to live in the dorm because it was cheaper, so she'd always had a roommate.

Hindsight was twenty-twenty. She probably should have tried to learn some of this stuff on her own.

"I read romance novels," she said quickly. "Dirty ones."

TJ cupped her cheeks and kissed her, gently at first, but then with more passion. It reminded her of the kiss by the campfire. It had rocked her world. That night she had gone back to the RV and wished for something...anything to offer her relief.

She'd run her fingers over her clit, adding pressure and pace—until she felt everything inside her seize up right at the pinnacle. She'd slid two fingers inside, shocked by how wet she was, but in the end, she'd only succeeded in making herself more frustrated, unable to get herself off.

"Turn around," TJ said when their lips parted. "Let Doug see you, kiss you."

She moved without thought, the fact she was topless no longer as mortifying as it felt just minutes earlier. These men cared about her, genuinely.

She'd had twenty-seven years to dream about this moment. Apparently, she was a shitty dreamer because the reality was far, far better.

Doug was waiting for her, his lips on hers before she even finished her twist. "I've waited for this moment for years," he confessed when they came up for air.

"Me too. Sorry I was such an idiot."

He pressed his forehead to hers. "You're the smartest woman I know." As he spoke, he leaned back enough that his eyes could travel downwards, allowing him to sneak a peek of what he'd already touched.

"Why don't we level the playing field?" Doug tugged his own shirt off with one hand.

"Oh yeah," she whispered as Doug revealed his six-pack, ranch-hand abs. "Wow."

He winked at her, clearly delighted by her praise.

She turned her head when she felt TJ moving behind her. Like Doug, he'd taken off his shirt. Rosalia had chosen the wrong profession. If she'd known there was so much eye candy available on ranches, she would have bypassed the lab and learned how to ride a horse.

"Lay down, Rosalia." TJ's hands were on her shoulders, pressing her to the mattress. She'd only just gotten into place when Doug grasped the waistband of her fleece pants and pulled them off.

She clinched her legs together—the response fueled by shyness and nervousness.

TJ lay down next to her. He was warm and big and hard all over. Doug claimed the other side, and any vestiges of chill left from her time out in the rain vanished.

Doug kissed her cheek, but she wanted more. She turned her head and he gave her a proper kiss, firm lips, open mouth, soft tongue.

As they kissed, TJ's lips took the time to do some exploring of their own. Tingles traveled all the way down her spine when he ran his tongue down her neck, over the top of her breast before settling at her nipple. He sucked it into his mouth, roughly, and her back arched.

"Shhh." TJ's breath felt cold against her overheated skin before he repeated the suction.

Through it all, Doug kept kissing her, causing a serious sensory overload. There was too much to feel and it was all amazing.

"I don't want to miss anything," she whispered against Doug's mouth.

He lifted his head. "What?"

"It's too many good things happening at the same time. It's all new and I'm struggling to keep up."

TJ chuckled. "That's a valid complaint."

She shook her head quickly. "I'm not complaining. I mean, I don't want anyone to stop or leave or..."

"I'm not sure one of your category-five twisters could drag me or Doug out of this bed right now, darlin'."

"Tell you what. Why don't TJ and I work together a little better." Doug glanced up at his friend with a wickedly sexy grin. "Boobs?"

She laughed even as she shivered. The sound died quickly when both men took one of her breasts in their hands, squeezing the plump flesh before lowering their heads and taking her nipples into their mouths.

"Fuck me," she breathed out.

"That part comes later," TJ murmured, his lips still against her breast.

Neither man skimped on the foreplay, and Rosalia felt an intense ache between her legs. She rubbed her thighs together, trying to find some sort of pressure that might give her release. Her hands rested on the back of each man's head as she ran her fingers through their hair. They were blocking her path, making it impossible for her to touch herself down there.

"God," she gasped. "I need...you to..."

TJ lifted his head first. "Touch you?"

She nodded, perfectly aware that her face was flushed again. But this time, it had nothing to do with embarrassment and everything to do with the sudden rise in temperature.

"Touch you where?" Doug teased as he ran his finger—too lightly—along her side. He was a champion tickler.

Her eyes closed as her hips thrust upward in silent invitation.

TJ's large, calloused palm gripped one of her knees. "Open up, Rosalia. Let us in."

Until he spoke, she hadn't been aware that her legs were still pressed tightly together. However, she didn't have to worry about following TJ's directions, because Doug grasped her other knee and they pulled her legs apart together.

Cold air hit her pussy and she gasped again. "It's so hard to breathe right now."

Doug kissed her quickly. "If you can still talk, we're not doing a good enough job."

There was no chance she could reply because TJ wasted no time taking advantage of her new position. His finger stroked her clit firmly, and she reared back against the pillows.

Every touch sent a shock through her. It was lightning, electricity, high-voltage currents. She could power a city at this rate.

Doug bent his head again, sucking her nipple back into her mouth as TJ shifted until he was kneeling between her parted legs. It occurred to her she was completely naked, open, exposed.

And yet she didn't feel the need or desire to cover up.

Especially not when TJ lowered his face to her opening and touched her clit with his tongue.

Doug must have read his friend's intent ahead of time, because his hand firmly pressed on her stomach, holding her to the bed so she couldn't rear up.

TJ's large palms spanned her inner thighs. Rosalia had the sense of being held captive, the sensation erotic as hell and fueling her already over-the-top arousal.

TJ pressed his tongue inside her and she squeaked, the sound prompting Doug's laughter.

"God, you're adorable," he murmured against her breast.

Any reply she might have made vanished when TJ pushed a finger inside her. Her inner muscles clenched tightly and for a second, she thought she might come. Was that possible? Because it sure as hell hadn't worked for *her*.

"Holy shit," she muttered.

"So tight and wet."

She lifted her head from the pillow to look at him, because she wasn't sure if he meant that as a good thing or a bad thing.

"TJ?"

He smiled at her. "You're beautiful, Rosalia, but that's not making this any easier."

She frowned, confused.

"Not sure how to do this without hurting you."

"You won't hurt me." The words were sure and strong because she believed them, all the way to the depths of her soul.

TJ moved until he was lying next to her again. Then he gestured to Doug.

"Should be you. You two are practically married, after all. Besides, I already got the first kiss."

Doug chuckled, but there was no denying he wanted what TJ offered when he shifted, coming over her.

He held himself up on bent elbows on the mattress, kissing her.

"I realize I'm fairly innocent, but shouldn't the jeans come off first?" she teased.

"Impatient."

She started to say it took one to know one, when he pushed himself off the bed. Rosalia would have watched the show when Doug shed his jeans, but TJ was there, kissing her again.

Rosalia wondered how she'd lived a lifetime without kisses. They were so powerful, so incredible. She revised her opinion about eyes being the gateway to the soul. It seemed to her that the way these men kissed her told the tale better, more accurately.

The crinkling of a wrapper caught her attention, and she turned her face away from TJ to break the kiss.

"Do you have to use that?" she asked.

Doug was sitting on the edge of the mattress, facing away from her. She got her first peek at his bare ass, but in his current position she couldn't see the rest.

He looked at her over his shoulder. "That's up to you, Rosie. I'm clean, but it has to be your call."

"I don't want you to use it. Don't want either of you to. I think…" She bit her lower lip, then just said it. "I want to feel you. Just you."

Doug tossed the condom on the bedside table, then turned, climbing back in the bed.

Rosalia tried to school her expression but failed, and Doug caught sight of her wide-eyed astonishment.

"Trust me, sweetheart. It's just average. Nothing earth-shattering."

TJ chuckled but didn't say anything else. A quick glimpse in his direction proved TJ was looking at the same thing she was.

She tried to read his expression, tried to find the word to describe what it was she saw on his face. Finally, she landed on appreciation…or…desire?

It sparked a suspicion.

"Have the two of you ever done this before? Ever shared a woman?"

Doug shook his head at the same time TJ said, "Of course not."

She didn't ask her next question, given their hasty responses. Rosalia might not know much, but she figured it might be a buzzkill to ask if they'd ever slept with just each other.

Doug resumed his position on top of her, TJ scooting over to give him more room. She wrapped her legs around his thighs as he reached down to place the head of his cock at her opening.

TJ ran his fingers through her hair, drawing her attention to him. "Moment of truth."

She smiled. "So it is."

Doug didn't wait to hear more, taking her words as permission.

They held each other's gaze as he slowly pressed in. She suddenly appreciated TJ's comment about her being wet and tight. The juices of her arousal were helping, but that didn't mean it wasn't a tight fit. Her inner muscles clenched, but she couldn't tell if that was to draw him in or push him out.

She gasped when something sharp gave way, and he slid in to the hilt.

It stung for a second, but it didn't take her body long to become accustomed to the invasion.

Doug held still within her, waiting. "Take your time, Rosie. I'm not going to move a muscle until you tell me it's okay."

She licked her lips, then nodded. "It's okay. Honest."

He retreated as slowly as he'd pressed in. The sweat on his brow and his somewhat pained expression proved he really was doing everything in his power to minimize her pain, to make this good for her.

After two slow thrusts in and out, every trace of soreness vanished, replaced by a hot and heavy need for more. More friction. More speed.

"Doug," she whispered. "Can you go faster?"

He swallowed heavily, her gaze drawn to his throat muscles.

"Are you sure?"

She reached around, gripping his ass cheeks and squeezing them. "Very sure."

He kissed her on the cheek, his sweet, beloved smile covering his face. They'd flirted for years, and Rosalia wondered how she'd managed to resist him for so long.

Doug's movements grew faster as he pushed deeper.

Rosalia lost track of place and time, all her attention focused on the magical feeling between her legs. She tightened her thighs around Doug's waist, and her hands fell to the pillow by her head, in absolute surrender, as her strength deserted her.

"Doug!" she cried out. "God."

Her eyes opened just in time to catch Doug looking over at TJ, who reached between them, his fingers finding her clit, stroking it.

The trigger pulled, her climax fired. Her back arched as she screamed, her pussy clenching.

Doug followed her over, his deep voice grunting out her name along with a stream of beautiful curses. "Fuck! Rosie. Jesus. Yes. God, baby…"

As her climax subsided, she drifted into a soft, boneless state. She'd never been this relaxed in her entire life. It was almost as heavenly as the soul-searing orgasm she'd just had.

Doug fell to her side, the two of them sliding apart in breathless laughter.

"*That* was worth waiting for."

Doug pretended to tip the hat he wasn't wearing, turning on his cowboy charm. "Thank ya kindly, ma'am."

Rosalia sighed happily, hoping this idyllic feeling never disappeared.

TJ reached out to place his hand on her stomach. "That's a pretty sound."

She hadn't forgotten him—God, how could she? He was sex incarnate—but she wanted a moment to revel in the first experience. "TJ," she started.

"We've got all night, darlin'. Or…" He paused, and she watched doubt creep in. "Or I can excuse myself if the bed's too crowded."

"What?"

"Hell no!"

She and Doug answered in unison.

"Well, alrighty then," TJ replied with a chuckle.

Doug stretched and stood up. "I need to see a man about a horse."

Rosalia giggled as he headed to the bathroom. She turned to face TJ.

"You're still wearing your pants." She didn't have a clue where this flirty woman was coming from, but she liked her, liked being her.

"That's right. I am. They're gonna stay on a bit longer, too. You sore?"

She shook her head, though her quick denial wasn't exactly the truth. She was definitely twinging in some new places. But not badly enough that she didn't want round two.

"Mmmhmmm." His low grumbled hum proved he didn't believe her.

"TJ, please. I really want this. Want *you.*"

He tilted his head as if considering that. Then he said, "Want is a pretty powerful thing. I feel it too. It's not as strong as need though, Rosalia. So if you start to feel the want fading and the need doesn't show up, you let me know, okay?"

She wanted to ask what happened if she never stopped wanting him. Or if the needing part not only showed up, but took root.

But that felt way too heavy a conversation to have right now. Everything he said drove home how little she knew about TJ. And she knew her ignorance about him was intentional on his part. He had been purposely

Light as Air

locking her out, holding her at bay, and she didn't know why.

But TJ wasn't wrong. Her desire for him, her physical wants, were too strong to resist. So she didn't.

"I'll let you know," she said at last. Quickly adding, "But I don't see that happening anytime soon. I was a twenty-seven-year-old virgin up until half an hour ago. There's kind of a lot I want."

He gave her a soft kiss on the cheek. "We're going to make every minute count, Rosalia."

That time she couldn't deny her suspicions. TJ was putting a timeline on this, had already figured out there would be an end to it.

She opened her mouth to call him out for it, but Doug came back into the room.

"Roll on your back, Rosie," he said. She noticed he had something in his hands.

"What's that?"

"Grabbed a warm washcloth." As he spoke, Doug gently tugged her legs apart and cleaned her. The heat from the soft cotton felt wonderful.

A tear escaped before she even realized she was crying.

Doug caught it with his fingertip. "Catching up to you?"

"I'm not sad."

Doug gave her that cherished grin that had her insides melting. "I know you're not. It was a special moment for you. Hell, for me, too. Something I'll carry with me until the day I die."

Doug always seemed to know the perfect thing to say at the perfect time.

He finished cleaning her up, tossing the cloth to the floor, before tugging the covers down and crawling beneath them.

104

She followed suit. The two of them were still naked, but TJ hadn't made any move to join them in that state.

Doug must have sensed the same reticence she did. "We're not kicking you out of this bed, TJ. It's the three of us in this. We're adults and we all made that decision. Not sure where your head is but get it back in the game. This isn't the Doug and Rosie Show anymore."

"Rosie and Doug," she corrected, pleased when TJ not only chuckled, but took Doug's words to heart. He stood up to shed his jeans and boxers.

"Oh," she whispered as she got her first glimpse of naked TJ. She'd been the slightest bit drowsy a few minutes earlier, but just like that, her body shifted from tired to take-me-now.

She lifted her hands in invitation.

He accepted, the restraints he'd put on himself suddenly loosened. She expected him to follow Doug's example, to cage her beneath him, but missionary didn't appear to be on his mind.

TJ twisted her until she faced Doug, lying behind her. His arms wrapped around her as he took a breast in each hand, plumping the flesh. His cock was hard and poking against her back. She started to understand why he'd suggested Doug go first. If Doug was right about being average, TJ was definitely above average.

Not that it mattered. Especially when he started kissing the side of her neck, his teeth nipping at her earlobe as if he'd devour her whole.

"God. That feels so good."

Doug watched them for a few minutes before jumping in. He stroked a loving hand along her face, and she sucked in a deep breath, overwhelmed by the utter adoration in his eyes.

"You pick, Rosalia," TJ said. "I can take you the way Doug did or from behind. Or you can crawl up on top and ride me. I'm not exactly a small man, and I don't want to do anything that hurts."

Rosalia pushed her hips farther back. "From behind." Now that she'd lost her virginity, she wanted to soak up every ounce of this experience she could, wanted to learn everything they had to teach her.

TJ's hands cupped her ass cheeks, gradually squeezing tighter until she squeaked. "Not sure I can be…"

Rosalia waited for him to finish, clueless as to what he was talking about, but when Doug replied, she realized his words hadn't been meant for her.

"You're not paying attention, TJ. Our Rosie isn't made of glass. She's all woman. And she wants exactly what you do."

She wasn't sure what that meant, but she didn't disagree. "He's right," she added breathlessly, silently hoping he was. She was out of her league here.

Whatever was bothering TJ was assuaged, because one minute they were lying back to chest, and the next he had a grip on her hips, dragging her up until she was on her hands and knees.

"Oh man. I'm taking advantage of that," Doug said, lifting one of her legs and sliding beneath her. "Easy access," he teased as his lips closed around one of her nipples.

TJ knelt behind her, gripping her hips with his large, firm hands. There was no denying he was a strong man. Really strong. Yet that didn't frighten her, didn't make her feel anything less than completely safe.

TJ ran his finger along her slit. Despite Doug's clean-up job, she was wet again, two of his fingers slipping inside with ease. She lowered her chest toward

106

Doug, the position elevating her ass toward TJ. She was hoping he'd get the message.

His fingers weren't enough.

When he continued to play, she started rocking back and forth, trying desperately to grab more of what she wanted, what he was denying her.

His free hand drifted from her hip to her clit and she jerked roughly, her complaints coming out louder than she intended. "Goddammit. Fuck me already."

TJ and Doug chuckled, but neither one of the bastards changed course.

TJ added a third finger to the two inside her, and while the added pressure felt good, it still wasn't enough.

Rosalia's body was on autopilot, her movements frenzied as she tried—to no avail—to get what she wanted from TJ.

"Please," she cried, the word coming out weakly. "Need..."

TJ pulled his fingers from her, and she could have sobbed with relief.

That response would have been wrong. TJ wasn't finished playing with her. And she stopped caring when he ran the tip of one wet finger around the rim of her anus.

"God!" He pressed in two knuckles deep, and Rosalia's arms failed to hold her up. It didn't matter. Doug was there to catch her. He cupped her head, his fingers tightening in her hair, as she rested her cheek on his chest.

She turned her face slightly, sinking her teeth into Doug's pec. He groaned, then said, "Fuck, man. You're turning her into a rabid beast here."

Rosalia was too far gone to laugh at the joke. TJ's finger had stilled and she'd had enough. Her patience was completely gone. She jerked back quickly, trying to push him in all the way.

He took exception to her trying to take control, slapping her ass just once. "Hold still."

In any other place or situation, that deep, do-as-I-say-or-else voice would have intimidated her.

This time, it bounced off her like a rubber ball and she pressed back again, harder, faster. TJ spanked her again, placing two firm slaps to her ass.

If he thought that was going to stop her, he was sadly mistaken. Between the heat and the sting and the unbearable pulsing between her legs, she couldn't stop *herself*.

"Fuck me," she yelled.

TJ shoved his finger all the way into her ass, just once, just enough to pull a loud groan from her. Then he withdrew all the way, gripped her hips and thrust his cock into her pussy with all the speed and force of a freight train barreling down the tracks.

Her back arched as he hit the spot. She detonated. Exploded. Shattered into a million shiny pieces.

TJ disregarded her orgasm, continued to fuck her as if it never happened, harder, faster. There was definitely going to be evidence of his grip on her hips tomorrow, bruises most likely. She couldn't wait to see them, to touch them and remember this.

Rosalia recovered quickly—what choice did she have?—and picked up his pace, rocking back as he slammed forward. Doug was holding her, his hands on her breasts as he pinched her nipples. She felt his hard cock, rejuvenated after their lovemaking, beating against her stomach with each thrust.

She reached down and grabbed it, running her hand over it, loving the way her unexpected grasp caught Doug off guard.

"Fuck, Rosie. Baby."

Those words morphed into grunts when TJ placed his hand on top of hers and the two of them jerked Doug off, even as TJ never lost his own beautiful rhythm inside her.

"I can't...stop..." she gasped, trying to breathe in a suddenly airless room.

"I'm coming." She felt Doug come, jets of the sticky hot stuff hitting her stomach, landing on his.

She fell next, her forehead dropping to Doug's chest as her body shook with white-hot pleasure.

TJ was the last, both hands returning to her hips as he jerked inside her two more times before her name fell from his lips in absolute reverence. "Rosalia. Beautiful Rosalia."

The three of them remained in place, the only sound in the room that of them struggling to catch their breath.

TJ moved first, withdrawing and standing, heading to the bathroom. The sound of water met her ears.

"My shower is too tiny for all of us. Or for even two of us."

"Probably better that way," Doug murmured, his voice heavy as sleep started to claim him. "Can't see you wet under hot water and not take you again."

TJ returned with a new washcloth.

Rosalia read the apology on his lips before he spoke a word. She stopped him. "Don't say a thing. That was amazing."

"You were a virgin two hours ago. I was too hard, too rough."

"Shh," she soothed him. "Let me sleep for a few hours and I'll let you do it all over again."

Doug chuckled, even though he never opened his eyes. "I'll take that deal."

The creases in TJ's forehead proved he wasn't as easily appeased. He was quiet as he gave her the gentlest of baths, running the warm cloth all over her as she fought to keep her own eyes open.

"Toss that over here when you're done," Doug mumbled. "Not sure I can stand up and walk just yet."

TJ went back to the bathroom, rinsing the washcloth out. When he returned, he walked to Doug's side of the bed and ran it over his friend's chest, cleaning off the evidence of their lovemaking.

Rosalia turned to watch them, studying the wariness, yet... God, what was it? Anticipation? Expectation? Desire? It pulsed between them, setting off some serious *Brokeback Mountain* sexual tension.

When he was finished, TJ placed the cloth on the nightstand and walked around the bed, crawling in beside her.

She fell to her back, clasping hands with Doug, who'd fallen asleep within seconds.

TJ faced her, his hand resting on her stomach.

"You're really okay?"

He obviously couldn't rest without more reassurance.

"You were there, TJ. You tell me. Did I look like I hated any part of that?"

Finally, the clouds cleared and he smiled. "Probably wouldn't use the word hate. More like a woman possessed. Starting to think it's a good thing you invited me and Doug to your bed. Not sure one man could satisfy you."

She giggled. "Are you calling me a sex maniac?"

He placed a soft kiss on her bare shoulder. "If the shoe fits..."

Rosalia started to toss another joke his way, but with his conscience soothed, TJ drifted off to sleep as easily as Doug had.

She spent about thirty seconds jealous of their ability to fall asleep so quickly.

That was as long as she managed to stay awake before joining them in dreamland.

Chapter Seven

"You okay?" Doug asked, walking up to him. TJ was looking at the crescent moon through the trees. It was a beautiful, clear night, all traces of the earlier storm completely gone.

TJ nodded, but didn't say more.

Doug had woken up a few minutes earlier, surprised to find just Rosalia asleep in the bed. She was the picture of peace and contentment, so he'd left her there, quietly slipping on his jeans and shoes to go in search of TJ.

Doug looked at his friend, worried. Had he misread what happened in that RV? Because if he had to pick his top three best nights ever, tonight would be at the very top.

"TJ? What's wrong?"

TJ glanced down at the cell phone in his hand. "Got a call from Sawyer. Came out here to take it so I wouldn't wake you all up. Thorn hit a telephone pole tonight, totaled his car. He's in the hospital."

"Jesus," Doug said. "Is he okay?"

"Yeah. Bump on the head, just a minor concussion. He was drunk as a skunk and Sawyer said that probably saved him from getting hurt any worse. He was most likely passed out when he struck the pole, so he didn't tense up."

"How long is he going to be in the hospital?" Doug tried to temper his tone, but right now, he couldn't feel anything but anger toward TJ's father. Tonight had been one of the best nights of his life. If TJ had to leave now...

"Sawyer talked to the doctor. They're going to hold him for a few days. Try to dry him out. If that's even possible. There's a rehab center over in Clarke. Sawyer offered him a deal. Check into the center or he'll make sure the judge gives him the maximum punishment, which would include a year of jail time."

"What did Thorn pick?"

"Didn't yet. Told Sawyer his head hurt too bad. Asked if he could think about it until morning."

Doug was grateful to his uncle for stepping in, for offering Thorn a shot at straightening out his life. Plus, it bought him time. Time to focus on what they'd started tonight with Rosalia.

"He'll pick the rehab. He'd be a fool not to, right?"

TJ grimaced. "Never known my dad to pick the easy way. Or the smart way. Doug, listen—"

"No," he interrupted. "You listen. You're not leaving."

The sound of TJ's determined, defeated sigh told him that was exactly what he'd been planning to do.

"I need to get home, need to sort out all this mess with my dad."

Doug crossed his arms. "Sounds to me like it's been sorted. He's going to be laid up in the hospital for a few more days. After that, he goes to rehab or jail. Might surprise you, Third, but you can't go to either of those places with him. Stay here. This is where you need to be."

TJ looked away from him, his gaze traveling back to the sliver of moon. "I'm not so sure about that."

"Don't. Don't do that, TJ. Don't try to make what happened tonight wrong in your head. No part of that was wrong."

"I'm not like you and Rosalia, Doug. I don't look at the world through rose-colored glasses. You can't always get what you want."

"Thanks, Mick Jagger. I'll tuck that wisdom away for later, maybe pull it out for something it actually applies to. It doesn't work here."

"Fine. You don't like that song? I'll quote another…from *Sesame Street*. One of these things is not like the other. Rosalia is a doctor. She's got her whole life figured out. She's smart, driven, passionate about her work. And you're the same…except for the doctor part." TJ flashed him a ghost of a smile at the harmless dig before it vanished again. "You know who you are and where you're going. You have a path and you're walking it. In the meantime, I'm nowhere. I'm nothing."

Doug recalled saying something similar to Jake after he broke his leg. He'd always defined himself by just one thing—his future with the rodeo. Jake had shown him a man was made of a hell of a lot more. That it was a man's failures, his losses, that determined who he was as much as the shit he got right.

Jake had been an expert on loss. He'd spent the majority of his life without the woman who held his heart. Misunderstandings and bad decisions had kept Jake's only son away from him for well over half of Viho's life.

"You're wrong, TJ. You're somebody. Hell, you're one of the most important people in my life." Losing Jake had opened his eyes to those who really mattered in his life. Doug didn't intend to take one second with them for granted, wouldn't fail to show the people he loved how much they meant to him.

"I had a bottle of whiskey in my hands," TJ said.

Doug frowned, utterly confused. "What?"

"That day you came by the house and told me to pack a bag. Told me about this job. I was sitting in the kitchen with a bottle of whiskey in my hands. I planned to drink it. The whole damn thing. Been thinking about this name of mine. My grandfather was a drunk, too. Did you know that?"

Doug shook his head. Apart from TJ talking about his grandfather being absent throughout Thorn's life, Doug didn't know a thing about the man.

"Yeah. He was an alcoholic. My mother told me. Said that it was in my dad's genes. Pretty sure she said that in hopes of getting me to understand, maybe even excuse my dad when he fell off the wagon. 'It's in his genes,' she would say. Like he couldn't control the impulse to drink because it was chemical, deeply ingrained in his physical makeup."

Doug wasn't sure how to reply to that. Mainly because he thought there might be some accuracy in that assessment. "I'm not sure that's a thing, but I suppose we could ask Rosie. She's the science mind."

TJ shook his head quickly. "I don't want Rosalia to know about Thorn. I pray to God she never meets him."

While he knew TJ meant his words in another manner, they went through Doug like a knife to the heart. Doug had gone to sleep a few hours earlier, dreaming of a real future with TJ and Rosalia. In his mind, their first night was going to stretch into forever.

TJ obviously didn't feel the same way, and Doug was reminded of the realization he'd come to back in high school. TJ never dreamed. Never let himself hope.

Now, like then, Doug refused to accept that. TJ was a good man, honorable, honest, caring, but he wasn't perfect. He had too much pride. And the inability to see a happy ending for himself. Doug was going to have to work overtime to start flashing what was really possible in front of him.

"You don't have that gene, TJ."

TJ lifted one shoulder, clearly unconvinced. "I would have drunk it, Doug. And I'm pretty sure once I started, I wouldn't have stopped. Spent too many years watching my dad fall into the stupor that comes from the booze. It makes him forget. I've got some things I'd like to forget."

"You're not a coward like him. You don't need to forget anything. It's the memories that make you strong."

"What if you're wrong? What if I'm a lot more like Thorn than you realize? What if it's in my genes too?"

Doug shook his head. TJ was nothing like his father, but TJ didn't give him a chance to argue the point.

"Did you know it was love at first sight for him and my mom?"

Doug walked over to the nearest picnic table, sinking down on the bench seat. He'd been best friends with TJ since they were five. And tonight, TJ was dropping bomb after bomb, revealing things he'd never shared. Doug hated knowing his friend had kept all this bottled up for so many years.

"No. I didn't know that," he admitted.

TJ came over and leaned against the table, looking out across the playground.

"My mom told me. She told me all kinds of things after she finished the chemo and the doctor told her it hadn't worked, that there was nothing else to do. It was like she had to squeeze a lifetime of revelations into a few short months. She wanted me to know her history, her story, wanted me to understand who she really was, so I'd have something to hold on to after she passed."

Doug swallowed against the lump forming in his throat and actually felt a little jealous of TJ. There were so many things he wished he'd taken the time to ask Jake. Questions he'd never have answered because he'd always assumed there would be plenty of time later.

"I'm glad she did that. Glad she told you so much."

TJ nodded. "Yeah. Me too. Mom told me about meeting my dad at a community dance. Her family had just moved to town and they had attended, hoping to meet their new neighbors and make some friends. Even though they'd only been in Compton Pass a short time, they'd apparently heard all about Thorn Nicholas, the town bad boy. He was always in trouble for smoking in the bathroom at school, driving his car too fast, stealing beer from the convenience store, cussing and fighting. She had been warned to give him a wide berth. My mom laughed when she told me that."

TJ's eyes were faraway and Doug suspected he was recalling that time, sitting next to her bed, holding her hand as she talked.

"She said Thorn took one look at her, asked her to dance, she said yes—and that was all it took. He cleaned up his act, desperate to win her heart. Which she said he'd had, the second she'd looked into those big baby blues of his."

Doug had never realized Thorn had blue eyes like his son.

"Anyway. They got married, had me, had a lot of happy years. Dad had a few bad episodes, fell off the wagon occasionally, but she always got him back on. It's funny. I get the feeling my dad was always kind of a dick, but for her, he hid it as best he could. He tried to change for her, for love, to be a better man."

Doug tried to make this description of Thorn match the man he'd grown up knowing. Like TJ, he had memories of Thorn being sober when they were in elementary school, holding down a job at the same lumberyard where TJ just quit. But he wouldn't say Thorn was ever a good guy. Even sober, he was strict, stern, always sort of angry. It was one reason they'd always played at Compass Ranch as kids, only hanging out at TJ's house when his dad was at work.

"I've never been to her grave," TJ murmured.

After so many years as friends, Doug really didn't think there was anything TJ could say that surprised him. That did. "Why not?"

TJ shrugged. "We never had any money for a headstone. I swore I wouldn't go back until I could afford to get rid of whatever marker the cemetery had placed there. She deserves better than that. Now…it's been so long…too long."

Thorn drank away the money he made, which meant TJ's paycheck went for mortgage and utilities and food, so there wasn't any left for the gravestone.

"You're not like your dad. Not even close."

"Think about it, Doug. The job at the lumberyard, the falling too fast, the," TJ swallowed hard, "the temptation of the liquor."

"You didn't drink it."

"I would have. I wanted it. Bad. What if I can't keep holding back this beast inside me? What if, in the end, I stop trying to fight nature and I just let it go?"

"There's no beast inside."

"The last thing I would ever want to do is hurt you and Rosalia. I'm pretty sure Thorn was Prince Charming to my mom in the beginning. But as the years

118

went by, he disappointed her more times than I can count. She forgave him because she loved him, because she always saw a better man. I won't do that to anyone. Won't let anyone down."

And suddenly Doug understood TJ's reluctance to date, the reason he had very few friends. Hell, Doug was his only real friend, and he knew why. Because Doug was as tenacious as a bulldog and he'd never let TJ push him away. Never.

"Did you know Rosalia's grandfather was killed by a drunk driver?"

Doug reared back. Jesus. Where was all of this coming from? "No. I didn't."

"My dad is always going to be in my life. Not sure there's any way around that. Which means, if we let this go any further, Thorn becomes a part of *her* life, a constant reminder of what she lost at the hands of someone just like him."

"Why don't you tell her about your dad? Give her the chance to make the decision of what she can handle and what she can't."

"You keep talking about this thing like it's a done deal. Forever."

"And you keep pretending it's not. You're not leaving, TJ. We're only just getting started with something real, something amazing. I won't let you walk away from that."

TJ snorted sadly. "Yeah, well, maybe you better wait to make any hard and fast decisions until I finish speaking my peace."

Doug pushed himself up and walked around until he faced TJ. He was tired of his friend looking away. He wanted him to see him, see his eyes, see how serious he was about every word he'd said. "Fine. Say the rest and then we're going back to that RV, back to bed with our woman."

TJ met his eyes and held his gaze. "If I stick around, this is going to be a little more complicated than we thought."

There wasn't a damn thing complicated about the three of them together in that bed, and Doug was ready to fight to the death to convince his friend of that. "Why?"

Something in TJ shifted—and that was when Doug saw it, understood, knew what came next.

Even before TJ said, "Because I won't just be touching her next time."

Doug wasn't so sure that was true of last time, but he let it pass. He hadn't had time to think about or process his feelings about TJ wrapping his hand around his dick and stroking him. Granted, Rosalia's hand had been in between, but the intimacy was still there. God, Doug hadn't expected to come a second time, let alone as hard as he had. TJ's grip had shoved him right over the edge Rosalia had driven him to.

Then, TJ had washed him off.

Doug had considered grabbing the washcloth from his friend, taking over the ablutions himself, but he didn't. He couldn't.

"You wanted to kiss me all those years ago, didn't you?"

TJ gave him a confused look, so Doug explained. "That day in my folks' living room. I tried to stand up, but the cast on my leg threw me off-balance. You caught me and…"

"I wanted to kiss you."

"Why didn't you?"

TJ rubbed his temple as if warding off a headache. "Seriously, man? For one thing, you aren't Bryant. Neither one of us is…"

"Gay," Doug said, when TJ appeared to struggle with the word. "Maybe not, but I think there's definitely some bi in both of us."

"You're the only guy I've ever wanted to kiss. Period. So I'm not even sure how bisexual I am. You ever been with a man?"

Doug shook his head. "Nope, but I didn't hate it when you jerked me off in there with Rosie."

"There's a big difference between not hating something and enjoying it."

Doug snorted. "I went off like a bottle rocket, so I'll let *you* decide which one describes me. You know you've got that Dom vibe going in the bedroom."

TJ gave him a lopsided grin. "Fuck, man. I just stood here and told you I'm afraid I'm like my drunk asshole of a father *and* I want to have sex with you, and you're all-in without blinking an eye. You Comptons are weird, unshakable."

"Do those two things go together?"

TJ shrugged. "Fuck if I know. They just seem to fit whenever I'm around your family. You see things different than most folks. And you roll with it. Let it be. Thorn…" His words faded away, but Doug didn't need to hear any more. He knew how TJ's dad felt about "faggots," as he so lovingly called them.

The first time Thorn had called Bryant that in front of him, Doug had shoved the drunk fucker across the living room. TJ had held him back, kept him from doing any real damage. Not because he was defending Thorn, but because the man was blackout drunk, unable to defend himself, and because TJ knew Doug would

121

feel guilty about beating him up in that condition...eventually.

He wouldn't deny it would have felt damn good at the time though.

"TJ, if you think that revelation is going to change my mind about you leaving, you're nuts. I want to have sex with you, too."

"Think it through, Doug. All the way to the end. What do we tell Rosalia?" TJ asked.

Doug sighed. It was one thing to invite a woman to join them for a threesome. It was another to start getting it on with the other guy at the same time. Rosalia was innocent when it came to sexual affairs—*damn* innocent.

"I think you should tell her the truth."

Doug and TJ turned in unison, both of them shocked to discover Rosalia standing at the edge of the shelter.

"How long have you been there?"

Doug understood the sudden tone of panic in TJ's voice as he asked the question. He was bound and determined to keep his family skeletons in the closet.

She shrugged. "I just walked up. Just heard Doug admit he wanted you. I might have been a virgin a few hours ago, but I'm not blind and I'm not stupid. I caught the vibes between the two of you."

TJ looked heavenward as if praying, then his shoulders slumped. "And that doesn't bother you? Freak you out? Piss you off? *Anything*?"

She gave them both an adorable grin accompanied by her sweet blush. "I think it's kind of hot, actually."

Doug laughed as he walked over and wrapped her up in a huge bear hug. He placed a kiss on the top of her head. "You're adorable."

"So adorable you both left me alone in that bed." There was no anger behind her words, just teasing.

"Hey, don't look at me. I was warm and cozy and happily naked next you. It was TJ who skipped out on us."

"This is crazy," TJ muttered.

"You want to stop?" Rosalia asked.

Doug tucked her close. "He doesn't."

TJ gave him a hard look, but he didn't refute his assertion. After a quiet, tense minute, his gaze drifted to Rosalia.

"I don't," he said.

Chapter Eight

TJ threw some water on the fire pit, dousing the flames. After last night's confessions, he'd followed Doug and Rosalia back into the RV. The three of them had undressed and, through some tacit agreement, gone back to sleep.

TJ had been grateful for the reprieve, for the extra time to gather his thoughts. Telling Doug he wanted him and actually doing the deed were worlds apart. He'd been too shaken by his dad's car accident, and too rattled by Doug's willingness, to start anything last night. Plus, Rosalia had been a virgin. Taking her so soon again after her first time would only have hurt her physically.

So they'd slept—him fitfully—then gotten up and found a nearby campsite to take refuge in until the next storm appeared on the horizon.

Justin and Eric had just retired to their pop-up camper, neither of them remarking about the fact he and Doug hadn't set up their tent. The confrontation during the storm had given them away, and the shift in their relationship status with Rosalia had been noticed.

Rosalia placed her hand on his back as he stood staring at the wet ashes.

"You coming in?"

He turned to face her, not liking the hesitance in her tone. She was clearly afraid he was pulling away, and that was a fear he hadn't meant to put there.

"Of course I am, Rosalia. There's nowhere else I'd rather be."

She gave him a smile, but he wouldn't call it a happy one. "Do you think you'll tell me your secrets one day?"

TJ drew in a deep breath. "I don't have anything worth telling."

She tilted her head. "I don't believe that."

"What's the holdup?" Doug stood in the doorway of the RV.

"Patience isn't his strong suit," TJ muttered, happy when Rosalia laughed. This time, there was joy.

"I'm not going to lie. I'm feeling impatient, too."

He chuckled as she wrapped his arm around her shoulders, the two of them walking to the RV together. TJ shared their excitement, their anticipation, but his was tempered by a fair amount of anxiety.

He'd never given his heart to another. Not once in his entire life.

And now, in less than a couple of months, he'd lost it to not one, but two people. The realization terrified him as much as it thrilled him.

This was easier for Rosalia and Doug. They hadn't been beaten down by life. They'd grown up surrounded by love and support. TJ knew all too well how tenuous happiness could be. How good fortune could flip on a dime.

Rosalia took Doug's hand as she climbed the three steps into the RV. Then she turned to look at him, the frown line reappearing between her eyebrows. He'd given something away with his face.

"TJ?"

He pushed the dark thoughts, the irrational fears away. There was no place for them here. For tonight—and as long as it lasted—he was going to adopt the optimism of his lovers. Live in this moment and pray that it dragged on for weeks, months, years. Forever.

TJ felt the spark of a dream, the small flash of a plan for the future.

He'd never let those desires catch flame and burn…until now.

He smiled as he climbed the stairs. Doug and Rosalia laughed when he walked right by them, waving his hand toward the bedroom to indicate they should follow.

"And he calls *me* impatient," Doug mumbled, saying it loud enough for TJ to hear.

TJ was about to show them just how impatient he could be. He walked to the side of the bed, shrugging off his T-shirt on the way. He had his jeans unbuttoned and the zipper halfway down before Doug and Rosalia even got into the room.

Rosalia's eyes widened with obvious delight.

He nodded his head at her as he stripped off his jeans and briefs. "Get undressed. Both of you."

Doug crossed his arms. "Alpha much?"

"Takes one to know one."

Doug didn't bother to deny that. Instead, he tugged his shirt off as well.

Rosalia stood in the doorway of the bedroom and watched them, making no move to shed any of her own clothing.

"Pretty sure TJ's not going to repeat himself, Rosie," Doug said, giving her a gentle reminder of what they wanted.

Her cheeks flushed. TJ longed for, as much as he dreaded, the day when she became so accustomed to them that she stopped blushing.

She slowly started unbuttoning her blouse. While she'd shed some of her shyness last night, that had only come when she was out of her mind with arousal.

Today, the timidity had returned.

TJ stood facing her, his arms crossed. His cock was thick and erect. He made sure she had a bird's-eye view. A quick glimpse across the bed proved Doug was in the exact same state, his dick rock-hard and ready to roll.

TJ licked his lips as he looked at it, then he glanced up. Doug was watching him. So was Rosalia. She'd stopped undressing, far too interested in the silent interplay between him and Doug.

"Not happy about your lack of focus, Rosalia." TJ took the three steps necessary to reach her. He finished unbuttoning her blouse, then made short work of her jeans, panties and bra.

She tried to hide herself, one arm covering her breasts as the other hand shielded her pussy.

TJ narrowed his eyes. "It's not going to work this way, darlin'."

He grasped her wrists, pulling them away from her body. Rosalia struggled to break free of his grip for just a moment before stilling.

"TJ," she whispered, clearly uncomfortable under his intense scrutiny. He didn't release her.

"You're beautiful, Rosalia. You don't have to be embarrassed."

Doug sat on the end of the bed and ran his hand along her side, prompting a shiver. "You don't have to hide anything from us."

"But," TJ said, "you do need to listen to us."

He used his grip to pull her toward the bed. Doug followed his intent, helping him to place her facedown over the edge of the mattress before resting his hand on her upper back.

"What are you—"

That was all she got out before TJ placed a quick slap to one cheek of her bare ass. It was nothing more than a tap. He treated the other cheek to the same.

Rosalia didn't even try to push herself up from the bed, even though he knew he'd taken her by surprise.

"Rosie," Doug said, leaning down to her.

She sighed contentedly. "I've read about sensual spankings before, and last night...when TJ...well... I always wondered..."

"Wondered what?" Doug prompted.

"If they would turn me on as much in real life as they do in fiction. FYI, they totally do."

TJ chuckled and then, because he couldn't resist, he slid his fingers along her slit. Sure enough, she hadn't lied. She was wet and warm. He took advantage of it, slipping one finger inside her.

Her legs parted, an invitation for more. He accepted, adding another finger to the first, thrusting them in and out several times as her breathing accelerated.

TJ had just withdrawn them when Doug took his turn. He added his own smacks to her ass. He peppered her with six or seven as she squirmed and gasped.

"God, yes," she hissed. "Please."

Doug lifted her until her knees propped her hips and ass higher, her upper body still resting on the bed.

He stood and bent over, running his tongue along her, from clit to anus.

"God!" she cried. "Doug."

Doug fucked her with his tongue, pressing it in and out as she white-knuckled the bedspread.

TJ watched, mesmerized by the sight of his lovers taking and giving each other pleasure.

Rosalia slid forward on the bed when the pleasure grew too much. Doug growled as she pulled away, clearly intent on grabbing her back.

TJ moved faster. He reached out and gripped the back of Doug's head, turning his face toward him. Before Doug could react, he covered his best friend's lips with his own, hungrily, almost angrily.

So many wasted years.

TJ had thought about this kiss since they were boys, always with guilt and fear. His father, the world's biggest homophobe, managed to tell him daily how wrong this was. How unnatural.

Thorn was a blind fool.

Doug's hands gripped his waist, his fingers digging in, holding him there even though TJ's clenched fist in his hair should've told him he wasn't letting him go anytime soon.

He plunged his tongue into Doug's mouth, drinking up his breath, his flavor. They parted briefly.

"You taste like our woman."

Doug was breathing heavily, the mention of Rosalia distracting him before they could resume the kiss.

She had flipped over onto her back, watching them. Her fingers had drifted to her clit and she was touching herself.

"Was that your first kiss?" she whispered.

Doug nodded. TJ, meanwhile, struggled to figure out what to do next. He wanted it all. Now.

Wanted to kiss Doug again. Wanted to climb over Rosalia's body and fuck her like a man possessed. Wanted to drive his cock into Doug's virgin ass.

And then he wanted to do it all again and again.

Forever.

The word kept slipping into his thoughts unbidden, burrowing deeper, putting down strong, impenetrable roots.

While her cheeks were flushed, it was clear that this color wasn't driven by shyness. She was aroused, ready. "I'm glad I got to see it."

Doug knelt on the bed, reaching down. She took his hand, let him pull her to a sitting position. He and Doug sat next her, flanking her.

Doug kissed her, taking her lips gently, almost reverently. When he released her, TJ was there to take his place. He jerked slightly when Rosalia, the mischievous minx, nipped his lower lip.

When they parted, Doug gripped the back of TJ's head, initiating their second kiss. There was more force behind this kiss than the ones he shared with Rosalia. TJ felt the need to offer her softness, adoration. The same didn't hold true for Doug. With him, it was primal. Animalistic.

They spent the better part of fifteen minutes in this tag-team style kissing. TJ started to suspect Doug and Rosalia would be happy to continue the same all night. He wasn't that patient.

He pulled away, pressing Rosalia to her back.

"Wait there," he said to his lovers. "I need to get something."

He returned to the front of the RV, grabbing his backpack. He'd made an excuse earlier to slip away to the store, where he'd invested in a big tube of lubrication.

When he entered the bedroom, he saw that Doug had shifted, caging Rosalia underneath him as they kissed. Doug's cock rested along her slit and Rosalia had her legs wrapped around his waist.

TJ took a moment to enjoy the view. This was exactly how he wanted them.

Reaching down to his jeans, he pulled a condom out of his pants, then knelt behind Doug on the mattress.

Doug started to shift to the side, but TJ placed a firm hand on his hip. "Stay there."

Doug looked over his shoulder, a slight grin painting his face when he spotted what TJ had gone to retrieve.

"Thought you needed shaving cream."

He snorted at Doug's sardonic tone. "Got some of that, too."

Doug blew out a long breath. "You're not always going to be the top, Third."

TJ lifted one shoulder. "Didn't think I would. But tonight…"

Doug, the eternal clown, knew how it was going down tonight. "Be gentle with me."

Rosalia giggled, the sound cut off when Doug's focus returned to her. "You think that's funny?"

She shook her head. "I think this is surreal, amazing, the best night of my life."

"Thought that was last night."

"It gets better every night."

Doug kissed her, as he tilted his hips just enough to drag his cock to her entrance. He slid in to the hilt with one fluid motion, provoking a sexy moan from their girl.

Once he was buried deep, he held the position for just a moment before coming back on his knees, dragging Rosalia with him. Rosalia peered at TJ over Doug's shoulder, winking at him.

Doug shook his head. "I saw that."

Stealing one more kiss, he broke away from Rosalia's lips just long enough to say, "Your turn," to TJ.

TJ uncapped the lubrication, pressing the tip of the nozzle to Doug's ass and squeezing a generous dollop inside.

Doug shivered. "Shit. That's cold."

"Give it a second." TJ pressed the tip of his finger in Doug's anus, prompting another shudder. Slowly, he slid his index in, adding a bit more lube on each return.

"Jesus," Doug murmured.

Glancing down, TJ saw Rosalia's hands wrapped around Doug's cock, giving him a hand job as TJ worked his ass.

"Good girl." TJ threw his own wink back at her when she grinned.

"He likes what you're doing," Rosalia whispered.

Doug groaned when TJ pushed a second finger in next to the first. "The two of you are going to kill me."

For several minutes, TJ worked to stretch Doug's ass, adding more lube and another finger. When he had three sliding in deep and easy, he withdrew and reached for a condom.

Doug gripped one of Rosalia's hips. "Flip over, beauty, and raise that pretty ass up."

Rosalia lost no time assuming the position, pressing back toward Doug until she'd taken his cock back inside. TJ couldn't see from his vantage point, but he sure could hear. They may have only had one night together so far, but he was already familiar with their sounds—the squeaks and sighs—that told him what was going on.

"TJ's going to fuck both of us," Doug murmured, his hands planted flat on the mattress.

Rosalia's face rested against the pillow and she sighed the words, "Oh God," when Doug ran his tongue along her spine.

Once he'd lubed up the condom, TJ took a steadying breath. He was struggling to keep hold of his own thoughts and feelings, too wrapped up in watching Doug and Rosalia. He'd been here just over a month and yet, these two people had taken over his world. He'd gone from nothing to everything in the blink of an eye.

That little voice in the back of his head that told him this couldn't last was growing fainter.

He placed the head of his dick at Doug's anus and blew out an unsteady breath. He wanted this—Jesus, he needed this—but that didn't mean he wasn't scared. He'd had too many years to think about what it would be like to be with Doug, too many nights of shutting out his dad's voice telling him two men fucking was unnatural, that they should be locked away from polite society.

God. It suddenly occurred to him that was the fucking voice that had *always* been there.

It was his dad's. Constantly telling him that life was shit, that there was no point in trying too hard because it would just sucker punch him in the gut when he least expected it. TJ didn't doubt that was what his father believed. Because he'd lost the love of his life to cancer when she was just thirty-three years old.

TJ didn't want that. Didn't want to die bitter, angry...alone.

He wasn't alone now.

He pushed the head of his cock inside, then waited.

The muscles in Doug's shoulders bunched. "Fucking tight," he said through clenched teeth.

"Okay?"

"Don't you dare fucking stop."

TJ grimaced, resisting his own body's instincts that clamored to take, to claim, to fuck. He had to go slowly, had to give Doug time. He pressed in another inch. Then another. It was a game of degrees, something that couldn't be rushed.

He didn't manage to suck in a lungful of air until he was there, fully lodged. Inside. Doug. He tried to wrap his head around the sensations. It was tight and slick and, fuck, heaven. How could anyone anywhere believe this was wrong?

TJ noticed how tightly he was gripping Doug's hips and forced himself to loosen his hold. "Sorry," he muttered.

Doug obviously hadn't noticed his hands, all his focus otherwise engaged. "You gotta start moving, man. I'm dying here."

Rosalia wiggled her ass in silent agreement.

His lovers.

His.

TJ tightened his grip again and gave into his own desires. Because he realized these two amazing, incredible, intelligent people wanted the same. He wasn't sure he deserved them…yet. But he was damn well going to make sure he got there.

He withdrew until only the head of his dick remained, then he thrust back in—with speed and strength. His motion propelled Doug forward, deeper into Rosalia, who gasped.

It became a battle of wills as the three of them fought to stave off their orgasms. None of them wanted it to end. When TJ felt himself getting close, he slowed the movement and made his thrusts shallower until he regained control.

Rosalia wasn't bothering with patience. She stroked her own clit, her first orgasm coming within minutes. TJ stilled as she cried out her pleasure.

Doug's body stiffened and he cursed. "Fucking hell, Rosie. So good. Killing me, baby." Somehow, he managed to ward off his own climax, probably because TJ had stopped moving. He didn't intend to give him that option the next time.

Rosalia took only a few seconds to recover once TJ started moving in Doug's ass again. The two of them picked up a rhythm, Rosalia pushing back as he pressed forward. Doug was trapped in between, and from his constant groans and moans and shudders, TJ was pretty damn sure he wasn't suffering from the placement.

The thought prompted a grin. Then he considered himself in Doug's place.

It was the wrong thing to do. His balls tightened, and he knew no force of nature was holding off this climax.

"Touch her clit, Doug. Make our girl come again. I can't—"

He didn't finish his words, didn't have to. Doug had Rosalia back at the precipice within seconds and the three of them unleashed on each other, moving together in a flurry of force and speed. It was clearly physics *and* chemistry at play. Rosalia could explain the science to them later.

"God. Yes!" TJ closed his eyes, his body racked with a pleasure so intense, it almost hurt. He came roughly, filling the condom, bottomed out in Doug's ass.

He lost track of Doug and Rosalia's responses, too blinded by his own bliss.

It was several minutes before he could find his way out of the white noise, clear the gray haze enough to see them again.

They fell like dominos. Rosalia went first, facedown on the pillow. Doug followed her, twisting at the last second to her side. TJ managed to remain upright, kneeling above them for only a moment more. He turned and fell to his back on Rosalia's other side.

He needed to get up, pitch the condom and clean up, but every ounce of strength was gone, his bones turned to mush.

Rosalia and Doug must have felt the same as neither of them moved, the only sounds their labored breathing. Finally, Rosalia flipped to her back, flopping like a fish on the shore to do so.

"Holy shit," she said.

TJ chuckled.

"I wish I had the strength to laugh," Doug said, his voice deep and sleepy. His friend was well on his way to passing out.

TJ's grin grew. He was tired too, physically worn out, but energized at the same time. "I take it that means you all loved that as much as me?"

"So much love," Rosalia whispered.

TJ knew she was talking about the act, but there was something in her tone that made him think she meant something else. Or maybe it was his heart that heard it differently.

Love was an emotion he had very little experience with. In his lifetime and up until this point, he'd loved two people. His mom and Doug.

Now…

He reached out and took Rosalia's hand, giving it a quick squeeze. Hers remained limp. Glancing over, he realized both his lovers were out, down for the count.

He stood gingerly, muscles stiff from the workout he'd just given them. After a quick trip to the bathroom, he returned to the room, leaning on the doorjamb to look at them.

All the reasons he'd given himself for why he should walk away fled. This was where he was meant to be.

TJ had never felt more certain of anything in his life. Reality be damned. He was stealing the fairy tale, keeping it.

Forever started tonight.

Chapter Nine

Doug glanced up from where he was editing a video at the table in Rosalia's RV and spotted Justin's truck driving toward the campsite.

Finally, he thought. He and Rosalia had been waiting for TJ to return all day.

So far, they'd only managed to launch their weather balloons prior to three fairly substantial fall storms, marking this as their least successful research trip to date. He knew Rosalia was frustrated by the lack of storms. After all, it was mid-November and they were quickly approaching the end of the line. If something didn't break soon, the entire three-month venture was basically a bust.

Of course, while the research had floundered, the romance had flourished. For six weeks, Doug had lived in a constant state of...well...ecstasy. He, TJ and Rosalia fell into bed every night, touching, kissing, exploring, learning each other's bodies.

But it was so much more than just sex. They were bonding emotionally as well, spending hours around Rosalia's small dining booth, talking, laughing, discussing everything from politics to religion to *Game of Thrones*.

They shared more on a personal level as well. He and TJ had stayed up all night a few weeks earlier, holding Rosalia as she talked about her cancer scare, the surgery, and her fear—though alleviated by her doctor and online research—that she might not be able to have kids.

A couple of nights ago, it was Doug who'd fallen apart, when it dawned on him that Jake had been dead six months. He couldn't count the number of times he'd reached for his phone during that period to call the man, to tell him about Rosalia. And TJ. Doug could almost imagine Jake's face when he dropped that bomb.

Not that the shock would have lasted for long. Jake had worked on Compass Ranch for well over forty years. Doug and TJ had shared a chuckle, though their eyes had been misty, as they'd tried to guess what Jake would say about them. TJ thought it might be something to the effect of Silas being a bad influence on them, showing them they didn't have to choose if they didn't want to. They'd heard Jake joke more than once about Silas being a greedy bastard, claiming two true loves instead of settling for just one.

Doug decided Jake's response would be something much simpler. In fact, he could almost hear the blunt old man harrumphing, then saying, "It's about time."

The best part, however, was TJ. Ever since turning that corner back at the beginning of October, he hadn't looked back. While he still hadn't talked to Rosalia about his dad's alcoholism—he was worried about her reaction, given her grandfather's death—he had shared quite a bit about his mother, telling stories about her that even Doug had never heard. He'd been struggling the last few years to understand TJ's unshakable need to remain true to the promise he'd made to his mother, but hearing him talk about her, seeing how much he adored the woman, was enlightening.

Doug and Rosalia had spent most of the day lost in their work. So much so, Doug hadn't even realized dusk had settled in on them until he saw the headlights of Justin's truck.

Rosalia was sitting across from him, her forehead creased in concentration as she studied the data they had acquired thus far.

"He's back."

She looked up, then out toward the road. "Good."

He and Rosalia had woken up later than usual, TJ already gone. Doug figured he must've left pretty damn early, considering he hadn't even heard him getting dressed. TJ and Justin had planned to run errands in a nearby town, stocking up on dwindling supplies.

Doug hadn't expected it to take them so long.

He and Rosalia walked outside, ready to greet him. Doug frowned when he saw the passenger seat empty.

"Where's TJ?" Rosalia asked when Justin climbed out of the truck.

Her question seemed to take Justin aback. "Gone. Didn't he call?"

Doug's chest tightened. "What do you mean, gone?"

"I dropped him at the bus station at the crack of dawn. He said he needed to get back to Compton Pass. Woke me up to ask if we could leave earlier than planned. Guess he figured it was no big deal for me to drive him since we were going to town anyway." Justin gave them a shit-eating grin. "Said you two were sacked out, dead to the world. Busy night?"

Justin and Eric had spent the last six weeks trying to wrap their heads around the fact that both Doug and TJ were sleeping in Rosalia's bed. It had been entertaining to watch them slowly put the pieces together without ever working up the courage to come right out and ask. Eric still blushed whenever the three of them emerged from the RV together, but Justin, true to form, had found his sea legs enough to start teasing them about it.

Rosalia looked around the campsite, then at Doug. "Do you think he left a note and we missed it? Did he tell you why he was leaving, Justin?"

Justin shook his head. "No. Said he'd wait until a proper hour, then call you from the bus station to explain."

Doug pulled his cell from his pocket, dialing TJ's number. He frowned when he heard TJ's ring tone in Justin's camper.

Eric descended, holding TJ's phone. "Hey, TJ," he called out, not looking up from the phone's screen. "Doug's calling you," he said with a grin.

Glancing around, Eric realized TJ wasn't there. "Where's TJ?"

"Why do you have his phone?" Rosalia asked without answering.

Eric pointed to the spot where Justin always parked his truck. "Found it on the ground there this morning. Figured it fell out of his pocket when he was getting in the truck. Tucked it in my jacket for safekeeping and forgot about it until it started ringing just now."

"He doesn't have a phone," Rosalia murmured.

Doug sighed. "That would explain why he didn't call."

"I don't understand why he would leave without talking to us, without saying goodbye."

There was the slightest bit of panic in her voice, and Doug knew where her thoughts were going. TJ had admitted to both of them that he'd been on the cusp of leaving several times in September because he'd felt like an interloper, like the one piece to the puzzle that didn't fit. They'd reassured him, and Doug had truly believed those initial fears had been alleviated.

"It's too soon to panic," Doug said. "I'm calling Sawyer."

"Your uncle? The sheriff? Why not just call your dad? Or brother?"

Rosalia had a point, but she didn't know about Thorn.

Of course, Compton Pass wasn't that freaking big. If something had happened, his whole family would know it. Sawyer had popped into his mind because Doug figured he'd have the firsthand knowledge. The only thing that would have dragged TJ from their warm bed this morning was Thorn. God only knew what the bastard had done this time, but Doug suspected it was bad.

He clicked on Sawyer's number without responding. It was up to TJ to talk to Rosalia about his dad, pride be damned. Doug intended to make sure that conversation happened as soon as they were all in the same state again.

"Hey, Saw. Did you call TJ this morning?"

He heard the tone of surprise in his uncle's voice when he replied, "Yeah. Sorry about the early hour. It was a hell of a night."

"What happened?"

"Didn't he tell you?" Sawyer asked.

"No. Caught a ride on an early bus with intention of calling me from there. He dropped his phone at the campsite."

"Not surprised," Sawyer said. "Poor guy was pretty shaken up. His dad left rehab and hitched a ride back home. Guess he figured he'd make up for lost time. Got blackout drunk and fell asleep with a cigarette in his mouth. Their house is gone, burned to the ground. Thorn's in the hospital, in rough shape. Smoke inhalation and second- and third-degree burns pretty much all over him."

"Fuck," Doug muttered.

"What is it?" Rosalia asked, stepping closer, concern written all over her face.

He reached out to take her hand, giving it a quick squeeze. "TJ left on the bus this morning. Figure he'll be rolling into the bus station in town anytime now. Think you could swing by and pick him up?"

Sawyer agreed. "No problem. Sort of surprised you didn't drive him."

"Would have if the prideful bastard had asked."

Sawyer chuckled. "Boy always did have more stubborn than sense. You heading back?"

"Yeah. I'll be on the road all night."

It was obvious his uncle didn't like that idea. "You sound beat, Doug. I'll get TJ. He can spend the night in your bedroom at the ranch. Jody and Lucy and my wife are itching to get their mothering hands on him. He'll be well-fed and sleeping between clean sheets in just a few hours. You get some sleep and head out at first light. Last thing I want to do is knock on your mama's door and tell her you fell asleep at the wheel."

His uncle had a good point. Doug knew his family. Knew they'd take good care of TJ until he could get there. "Sounds like a better plan than mine. Will you ask him to call me when he gets there?"

"Will do."

He and Sawyer said their goodbyes.

"Well?" Rosalia prompted.

"His house burned down." That was far from everything, but Doug was standing on shaky ground. A few hours ago, he'd been on top of the world, but now he was worried. TJ had always taken that vow to his mother very seriously, and Doug had convinced him to toss it aside, to leave town and his dad and go on an adventure.

While TJ had been all-in the past few weeks, how would he feel about things now? Doug knew his friend well enough to appreciate TJ was bound to feel guilty as hell. But he didn't know how TJ would react to that guilt.

Would he try to push Rosalia and Doug aside, pull away from them?

He might try, but Doug was made of sterner stuff. What TJ had in stubbornness, Doug had in persistence. He intended to be the winner at the end of this battle.

"Oh my God. Was his dad home?"

Doug nodded. "He's in the hospital. Burns. Smoke inhalation. My family is going to put TJ up for the night."

"We can leave right now. Take the RV and get Justin and Eric to follow with the other two vehicles."

"Uh, Rosie?" Eric interrupted, holding out his phone. "We've got activity on the radar. Conditions lining up. Could be a twister. Not too far from here. Two-hour drive."

"No," she whispered.

"I wasn't going to leave until morning," Doug said, too many things hitting him at once. He was worried about TJ, still waffling on racing halfway across the Midwest tonight, and now this.

"I, um…shit." Rosalia looked just as torn.

"You have to go," Doug said, letting her off the hook. "It's your job, Rosie. You don't have a choice."

Her expression proved she already knew that. "We'll go. Set off the balloons, get what we can. As soon as the storm passes, I'll follow you to Compton Pass. With any luck, I'll only be a day or two behind."

It was a good plan. Except for the part where she was rushing off to chase tornadoes without him. If he could rip himself in half and travel in two different directions, he'd do it in a New York minute.

He looked at Justin and Eric. "Take care of her."

Eric nodded earnestly, and he expected Justin to make a joke. Instead, his friend walked toward him and patted him on the shoulder. "Gonna guard her with our lives. You know that, man. TJ needs you. I mean, I can't imagine what he's going through. Lost his home and his dad in the hospital. Times like that when a man needs his best friend."

It was the most serious thing Justin had ever said to him. And it was exactly what he needed to hear.

"You're right."

He helped the rest of the team pack up the campsite, then watched as Rosalia led the way in her RV, Justin and Eric following in their truck. It was a chilly night, and he and TJ hadn't bothered setting up their tent since following Rosalia to her bed.

"Fuck it," he muttered. If he hadn't stayed up half the night last night, making love to Rosalia and TJ, he'd be in a better state and able to drive. As it was, he knew his uncle had been right to suggest he wait. He didn't have it in him to drive ten hours straight in the dark. He'd sleep in the cab of his truck and take off first thing in the morning.

Before he did that, though... He reached for his phone and searched for James in his contacts. He had a few phone calls to make, and he was going to start with his brother, then his cousin Jade. Then maybe Vaughn.

He was a man on a mission—and he was bringing in the Compton recruits.

Chapter Ten

TJ sat on the stump of an old tree he'd chopped down a couple of years earlier due to disease and looked at the pile of wet ash in front of him.

He hadn't owned much, but everything he had was gone now. Childhood toys, old sporting equipment, the ancient video camera Seth had let him keep. Everything was just…gone.

TJ glanced at the bottle of whiskey in his hands.

"You going to drink that?"

He jerked, surprised when he saw Austin, Bryant and James walking toward him. He hadn't even heard them pull up in Austin's truck.

TJ shook his head. "No. I'm not." He'd found the damn thing in a bush near where their front porch used to be. He could only assume his father had hidden it there to keep TJ from dumping it out, and then forgotten about it. TJ didn't have a clue how it had survived the fire and the firefighters and all the equipment they'd used to douse the flames.

James stepped next to him, studying what was left of the house. He worked as a volunteer firefighter in Compton Pass, so TJ assumed he'd been part of the squad that had worked to save his home.

"Doug called. He's on his way home."

TJ frowned. "What? Why?"

James rolled his eyes. "Because he's worried about you. Talked to Sawyer last night, who filled him in on the fire."

TJ was running on fumes right now. Two nights ago, he was up until the wee hours, losing himself in Rosalia and Doug. He'd only managed to grab a few hours of shut-eye before Sawyer called to tell him about the fire. He had considered waking Rosalia and Doug to explain, but it was barely four a.m., and he knew they'd want to come with him. He couldn't do that to them. This was his mess to fix. So he'd bought a bus ticket online, packed up his stuff and gotten Justin to drop him off. He figured he'd call to tell them where he was once he was well on his way home. They could finish up the last few weeks of the research stint and then…

It was the "then" he hadn't been able to figure out. A lifetime spent living in the moment had fucked up his ability to see much farther than the end of his nose.

He hadn't managed to sleep a wink on the bus. A mother and her small child were behind him, and the kid kept wiggling, kicking the seat. He'd spent last night dozing restlessly in a chair by his dad's hospital bed. His dad, drugged to the gills for pain, had never opened his eyes, never realized he was there.

Now, his eyes were dry and scratchy, his head hurt, and he was too tired to contemplate his next move.

"I was going to call him to explain, but I lost my phone."

Austin walked over to the rubble and kicked his boot through some of the charred wood. "Doug told us. They found it at the campsite, figure it fell out of your pocket."

Bryant squatted down, picking up what looked like a melted record from a pile of ash. "Sawyer went to pick you up at the bus stop, but he must've just missed you. Seth and Jody were hoping you'd stay at their house. Where did you go?"

"I walked to the hospital."

Austin's brows flew up. "That's a good three, four miles."

He shrugged. "Needed the time to think."

"You didn't have enough time on the bus?" James asked sardonically.

TJ snorted.

"How's your dad doing?" Bryant asked.

"He'll live." TJ noticed the way Bryant winced at his tone. If he weren't so fucking sick and tired of this shit, maybe he'd summon up some guilt over sounding upset that his dad was still alive.

Right now…he couldn't temper his anger. He looked at the scorched shell of the house he'd grown up in and recalled Rosalia's locket from her grandmother. While there hadn't been much of his mom's left in the house, what few things that had remained—some costume jewelry, the terry-cloth robe she'd worn almost exclusively the last couple of months she was alive, and her sewing kit, were gone for good.

All because his dad had decided rehab wasn't for him.

"How did you know I was here?" TJ asked.

"Sienna called me right after she dropped you off," James replied. Sienna was Doug and James's older sister. She and her husband, Daniel, lived in their own place on Compass Ranch. Quite a few of the family had settled on the vast property that had been JD Compton's back in the day. Doug's grandfather had been dead for well over twenty-five years, but he was still a legend in town, someone remembered, revered.

Sienna was a nurse at the hospital, but she was on maternity leave, and she'd stopped by the hospital while running errands because one of her colleagues hadn't had a chance to see the baby yet. She had seen him there in his father's room, eyes barely open and so numb he couldn't feel his own body.

She'd taken one look at him and told him to get his ass in her car, that she was taking him back to Compass Ranch where he could crawl into a clean bed and sleep. He may have been an only child, but in some ways, it felt like the Compton kids were his siblings, Sienna and James treating him like another little brother.

They had almost been back to the ranch when he'd asked her to change direction, to take him to his house. Sienna had protested, promising to bring him back later, but he'd insisted.

She must have called James the second he shut the passenger door behind him. It hadn't taken Doug's brother long to rally the troops.

"So what's the plan?" Bryant asked.

TJ wasn't sure if he meant today or in the future, but he didn't have an answer either way so he shrugged. "House had belonged to my mom's parents. She and my dad had been renting an apartment in town, but they moved here after her folks passed away. There's no money to rebuild, so I guess I'll try to find a place to rent."

TJ didn't mention Doug and Rosalia. He knew Doug had told his brother and cousins about Rosalia, but they'd agreed not to mention their change in status until they were all together and they could do it in person. It was one thing for straight Doug to tell his family that the girl he'd been madly in love with for three years had finally admitted she loved him back. It was another to announce he'd come out of the closet for TJ and the three of them were shacking up, threesome-style.

Not that Doug's family would blink an eye at that. But...Doug wanted to have that talk face-to-face with TJ present, and not through a video call.

"And your dad?"

TJ sighed. "I don't know. It's going to be a bad recovery for him. He was seriously burned. Doctor mentioned there would probably be several surgeries, skin grafts, stuff like that. He's not getting out of the hospital for a while." He didn't bother to add he didn't have a clue where that money was coming from. Neither of them had jobs at the moment and no health insurance. The well just kept getting deeper and deeper, and TJ feared he'd never find the bottom so that he could start pulling himself out.

He'd told Doug—warned him—that signing on with him was a bad bet. TJ was suddenly buried under a heap of debt with a badly scarred alcoholic to care for. This was what TJ had been waiting for. The sucker punch had come and right now, it felt like a fucking KO.

"You need sleep, man," Austin said. "You look wrecked. Pretty sure things wouldn't feel so overwhelming if you weren't so tired."

TJ didn't share that optimism.

And he didn't have the energy to move. Not even to James's truck. Glancing over at the vehicle, he noticed another one coming down the driveway. It was Grand Central Station, with the number of Comptons piling up around him.

This time, it was Jade climbing out of her car. She waved when she saw them all watching her.

151

"How did you know we were all here?" Bryant asked.

"Sienna called me," Jade replied.

"Didn't realize there was a phone chain attached to my name." TJ instantly felt bad for the bitterness in his tone. "I mean…God, I'm sorry. I didn't mean that to sound so shitty."

James placed a strong hand on his shoulder. "Come back to the ranch with us, bro."

"Nope." Jade reached down to him, holding out her hand. TJ took it instinctively, letting Doug's small-framed, tough-as-nails cousin pull him up. "You're coming with me first."

"Where?"

She paused, considering his question, then shook her head. "It's a surprise."

He could see the curiosity on the faces of the other men, but they all knew Jade too well, knew if she said she wasn't telling them, she wouldn't.

"I guess we'll see you back at the ranch in a little while then," James said as they all walked back to the two vehicles. "Doug should be pulling in about dinnertime."

James didn't mention Rosalia, but he knew that if Doug was coming, she was too. Which meant he'd royally fucked up her research project. TJ would have to borrow a phone once he got to the ranch to call Doug, to see if he could convince them to turn around.

He rubbed his eyes. Yeah. That wouldn't happen. If Doug's nose was pointed home, he wasn't going back no matter what TJ said.

He climbed into the passenger seat, relieved when Jade pulled out onto the main highway without talking. He was out of words, tired of trying to come up with answers to unsolvable problems.

Austin was right. He needed sleep. He tried to do the math and figured out he'd only gotten four hours of sleep in the last three days. Jade drove in silence, making her way into town.

He frowned when she pulled up in front of the church. TJ wasn't exactly a praying man.

"Uh, listen, Jade, church is a nice idea and all, but—"

"Not the church." She pointed to the adjoining cemetery. "There."

TJ swallowed heavily and shook his head. Jade had a better chance getting him into the sanctuary. "No."

"Doug called last night. Said he thought it was time you and your mom had a chat."

He continued shaking his head, making no move to leave the car.

"I used to come here all the time when I was younger, a teenager," Jade confessed. "I always came on my birthday to visit George." Jade had been a twin. However, her brother George had died in childbirth.

"I didn't know that."

"Not many people did. I know it might sound silly. Sitting alone beside a grave, just talking to the air, but I always felt like George was listening. And even though he never directly spoke to me, he always found a way to make sure I left—every single time—with the answer I'd been looking for. You need to talk to your mom."

TJ wasn't aware of the tears streaming until one plopped off his cheek and hit his collarbone. He knuckled them away.

"Come on. Even if you don't want to talk, there's something you need to see." Jade was out of the car and halfway across the street before TJ could protest. He got out of the car, simply because he was too tired to figure out what else to do.

He followed her down the path, past countless graves, surprised that she knew exactly where his mother lay.

When she stopped in front of a beautiful granite headstone, he thought perhaps she was taking a second to say hello to George.

She looked at him as she pointed to the stone. "Take a look."

TJ felt a piercing pain roar through his heart when he read his mother's name.

Janet Elizabeth Nicholas.

Below the dates of her birth and death were the words, "Beloved wife of Thorn, adored mother of TJ."

"I don't understand. Where did this come from?"

"Doug called me in early October. Asked me to order it. The groundskeeper just placed it late last week. It's lovely, isn't it?"

TJ gave up trying to hold back the tears.

He'd been here one time, and that was the day they'd laid his mother in the ground. He had stood here, Thorn on his right and Doug on his left, and he'd never shed a damn tear. Now, the floodgates had been opened and there was no holding back the sorrow.

Jade reached into her purse and pulled out a small packet of tissues. He grinned through the tears when he saw them, recalling that his mother always carried the same package in her purse as well. He took them gratefully.

"I'll leave you two alone. Take your time," Jade said. "I'm going to do some window shopping on Main Street, maybe step into Sterling's jewelry shop to see what's new and say hi."

She started to walk away but stopped when he called out her name.

"Jade."

154

She turned toward him.

"Thanks."

Jade smiled. "I just placed the order. Doug paid the bill. He loves you. We all do. I know sometimes you feel lonely, like it's you facing a cruel world, but I hope you know…you're never alone. You'll always have Doug, and by extension, the crazy lot of us. You can decide if that's a blessing or a curse."

Jade always found a way to make him laugh with her straight talk.

TJ watched her walk away, waited until she was through the gate and back on the sidewalk before he turned his attention back to the grave.

He dropped to his knees and bent his head. Jade had suggested he talk to her, so he did.

"I'm sorry I haven't been here before now, Mom. I wanted to, I swear. I think about you every day." He swallowed hard, trying to dislodge the boulder-sized lump that had his voice sounding thin, strained.

"I know I told you I'd look after Dad. I tried to keep that promise." The tears started falling again. "I failed you. Failed him. I'm so sorry."

For several minutes, he cried out his grief, the agony he'd felt over losing her. And the house. And even his father. He'd tried for so many years to be worthy of her, tried to take over and do all the things she couldn't. Cancer had robbed too many years from her and for so long, TJ thought he could hold on to her memory, could make that tragic death okay by simply granting her dying wish.

Take care of your father.

His body shuddered roughly as the tears started to dry up.

Then something came to him. Something he'd forgotten. Words that had been lost to him until that minute.

And take care of yourself, my precious son. Find your happiness, and I will be happy.

TJ tried to figure out where those words had come from, where they'd been. For a second, he wondered if she'd actually said them, or if he was merely delusional from a lack of sleep.

He closed his eyes and let himself slip back to that bedroom so many years ago. Her breathing had become more labored, the death rattle, he'd heard it called. She'd been drifting in and out of sleep for several days, the time she was awake growing less with each passing hour.

TJ had been dozing on the chair next to her and she'd stirred, her hand moving in his. He had been surprised to find her eyes open, her gaze focused clearly on him after so many days of hallucinating due to the morphine.

She'd licked her dry lips and he'd leaned close in order to hear her whispered words. "Take care of your father. And take care of yourself, my precious son. Find your happiness, and I will be happy. Promise me."

"I promise," he'd said. But he had only remembered the first part of the vow.

For twelve years, he'd tried to hide the booze, picked his dad up from the bar when he was too drunk, paid the bills. He had done his best to follow through on his promise…but the truth was, Thorn didn't *want* to be cared for. He was hell-bent on following his wife to an early grave.

That was his decision. More than that, it was his right.

TJ was finished.

He'd get his dad into a care facility, he'd get a job—even back at the lumberyard if he had to—to pay the medical bills, but once his dad was back on his feet, he was on his own.

TJ was going to spend the rest of his years accomplishing the second part of his promise. The one he'd forgotten. The one he'd *truly* failed on…up until October.

He smiled when he thought about Rosalia and Doug.

"You'd love Rosalia," he whispered to his mom. "She's beautiful and sweet, just like you. And Doug grew up to be a strong, smart, capable man. You always said he was 'good people,' just like his family. I'm happy with them. Really happy. So maybe…" He placed his hand on the cold, soft grass in front of her stone. "Maybe that will bring you some happiness, too."

Jade was right. There wasn't a sound in the cemetery, yet he'd discovered the same peace he hoped his mother had found.

"I'll be back soon," he promised. "I won't stay away so long this time. I miss you every day, Mom. Love you."

TJ walked back to the street, but Jade was nowhere to be found. He considered seeking her out at Sterling's, but changed his mind halfway there, bypassing the jewelry shop, heading toward another store instead.

Vaughn looked up from some sketch he was working on when the small bell that hung above the door to Cowboy Ink jingled.

"Hey, stranger. Heard about the fire. Figured you'd be heading back to town. You doin' okay?" Vaughn asked.

Compton Pass was a small place, which meant everybody knew everyone else…and their business.

"Yeah. Bit tired, but hanging in there. Jade's down visiting with Sterling and she's my ride. Thought I'd come…" TJ wasn't sure why he'd come here. It had been an impulsive decision. His eyes landed on the sketch Vaughn had been doing, and whatever he'd planned to say vanished. "Whoa. That's amazing. Is that going to be a tattoo?"

Vaughn slowly placed his hand over the drawing, uncomfortable for some reason. "Um, yeah. Shit."

TJ frowned, completely flummoxed until Vaughn said, "I'm working on something for Doug. He called last night from some campground in the middle of God knows where. Got the impression he was worried about you and struggling to sleep. Called me to see if I could work on a mock-up for him. Something like Austin, Bryant and James have."

"They all have tattoos?"

Vaughn grinned. "Yeah. Austin sort of got the ball rolling after Jake passed. They look a lot like the ones their fathers got from my dad."

Snake had been the local tattoo artist, passing his talent and the business on to his son.

"You think I could see it?" Neither he nor Doug had any tattoos. For TJ, it was a case of never having money for something like that. He'd never thought to ask Doug if he wanted one somewhere down the road.

Vaughn paused for a second, and TJ realized what he'd just asked. "Never mind. I'm sorry. You're right. This is Doug's deal. It's private."

"It's not that. Doug already said he was going to show you the mock-up before he got it. Said he wouldn't put a drop of ink on his skin if you or Rosie hated it. It's just…" Vaughn sighed and turned the sketch around. "Here. Take a look. Maybe you can tell me if I'm on the right path. It's not finished yet, but it's close."

TJ gasped as he studied the drawing, his eyes flying over all the features, visually taking it apart section by section so he could soak it all in.

There was a compass that was very similar to the one Snake had put on Seth's back, as well as on Doug's uncles. TJ had caught glimpses of them during scorching summers when they all worked shirtless. There was a silhouette of a ranch hand that looked like Jake—that part had TJ's chest tightening. Of course, Doug would want to include a tribute to the man who'd meant so much to him.

The entire thing was surrounded with lines that gave the illusion of air, a twister, intertwined with film reels. It was that concept that tied the whole thing together to make it look like one composed unit. That was Vaughn's true talent. Taking so many ideas and creating a single portrait.

TJ could look at this tattoo for years and probably still not see all the nuances—and as he thought it, he saw something he'd missed. Etched in the air and done in a flowy script that mimicked the other lines were Rosalia's initials.

And his.

He snorted out a laugh. Jesus. Only Doug would ask to have something permanently tattooed on his back when absolutely everything between them was up in the air...literally and figuratively...according to this sketch.

Vaughn grinned at his response. "You like it?"

TJ nodded. "It's amazing. Perfect."

"Really? *All* of it?"

Vaughn was clearly digging for juicier details. "All of it. Does Bryant know about us?"

Vaughn shook his head. "Nah. Doug swore me to secrecy. Said you were going to talk to his family together. That still the case?"

TJ smiled, his future looking crystal clear for the first time in his life. "Yeah. That's still the case."

"And what about your dad?" Vaughn knew firsthand how big a homophobe Thorn was.

"He'll either deal with it or he won't."

Vaughn grimaced. "Spoiler alert. He—"

"Won't," they said in unison, laughing.

"I better go. Jade's probably wondering where I disappeared to by now. You think you might do a sketch for me? I'd like something similar, with the air and the film and..." As he spoke, he thought of his mom. He'd want to remember her somehow in his tattoo.

"Sure thing. Call me later in the week and we'll talk over the concepts."

"Thanks."

TJ was still dog-tired, but there was no denying he felt about a million pounds lighter than he had an hour ago. Jade was just coming out of Sterling's shop as he approached it.

"Okay?" she asked.

He smiled and nodded. "Better than I've been in a long time."

Her delight was palpable, and it simply added to TJ's newfound happiness.

"Can I ask a favor?"

Jade nodded. "Of course."

"I'd like to make one more quick stop before we head back to the ranch."

"Sure thing. Where to?"

"The hospital."

Jade sighed. "You sure you want to tackle that right now?"

He nodded. "Feel the need to make a clean sweep. A fresh start."

"Can't argue with that."

She dropped him off at the door and said she would chill in the parking lot, play a little Toy Blast on her phone, while she waited.

TJ took the elevator to his father's floor. This time, his old man was awake, and his scowl when he spotted him in the doorway was evident even through the bandages on his head.

When he spoke, his voice was hoarse, gravelly from smoke. "Came back, huh?" Thorn said, coughing violently.

TJ nodded. "Yeah. Sawyer called me about the fire. House is a total loss."

"It was a fucking dump anyway."

TJ couldn't disagree. When his mother had been alive, it had been a warm, comfortable home, the kind of place where a loving family would create a lifetime of memories. That atmosphere died when she did.

"So you ran off with your boyfriend, huh?" his dad taunted, sounding ridiculously like a middle-school bully.

TJ could never go back to being his father's keeper. He'd figured that out at the cemetery, but his father's vitriol, his hate, made it simpler to walk away.

"Yeah. Actually, I did. Doug and I are together now. We're in love with a beautiful Italian girl named Rosalia. I'm hoping to make a family with them."

His father's eyes narrowed to angry slits. "Fucking faggots. Always knew you were a queer. You're a goddamn disappointment. Thank God your mother died before she saw what you turned into."

161

"Don't ever talk about my mother again. If *anyone* has disgraced her memory, it's you."

That comment hit, but it didn't stick. His father was too far gone to ever admit fault. "Get outta here. Go join the Compton freak show. Every single one of you is gonna burn in hell."

TJ wasn't sure what he'd expected. No, actually, this was exactly what he'd expected. But he clearly had too much of his mother in him. There had always been a small part of him that hoped for better, prayed Thorn would change. Those days were over.

"Goodbye, Dad."

Thorn snorted and turned his head away from him. "You're dead to me."

"So be it." TJ walked out of the room. If the man had given him one fucking opening, said one decent thing, TJ never would have left him that way while he was so obviously in physical pain, but any drop of kindness that might have remained, evaporated. It was done. The ties severed.

TJ couldn't summon an ounce of sadness. He'd said his goodbyes to both his parents today, and now, he was looking forward to starting a new family.

Jade was there when he returned. "That didn't take long."

He lifted one tired shoulder. "It's over." That was as much explanation as he had to give. There was nothing more to say.

"Good. And now," she said, making it clear there would be no debate, "you're going to the ranch and to sleep. From the looks of you, I'd say about twenty-four hours should do it."

He offered no argument.

Chapter Eleven

Doug sat by the bonfire with his cousins and tried to relax. TJ was inside the house, in his bed, sleeping like the dead. He had wanted to wake him up when he'd arrived home a few hours earlier, but no less than four family members blocked him, telling him the poor guy had been exhausted, and there was nothing Doug needed to say to him that couldn't wait.

Doug didn't completely agree, but he went along with it. However, if TJ didn't wake up within the next hour, Doug was dragging his ass out of bed regardless of his family's interference.

Fortunately, he'd shown up on a busy, big day for his family. Bryant had earned his doctorate, and the entire Compton clan was in a celebratory mood.

With Bryant settled down with Vaughn, and James and Ivy, as well as Hayden and Austin all partnered up, he was the last Compass boy facing an uncertain future.

He'd had six weeks of his ideal time away from reality with Rosalia and TJ. Now she was back chasing her storms, without him to protect her, and God only knew where TJ's head was at the moment.

Vaughn tucked his arm around Bryant and teased Doug about being jealous of them. He tried to deflect, tossing back a comment about being a bachelor, the joke falling flat.

There was nothing he wanted less than to be single. He'd told Vaughn about him and TJ and Rosalia. So far, he was the only one in Compton Pass who knew Doug's "new relationship" included three people, not just two.

When Bryant leaned closer to Vaughn and said, "I found Vaughn a long time ago. It just took forever to work things out. That could be the same for you," Doug wondered if Vaughn had spilled the beans.

Vaughn covertly, subtly shook his head, and Doug sighed. "I'm not that patient." He reached for another beer and glanced at his phone. Forty-five more minutes. He was giving TJ forty-five more minutes to sleep.

Sterling carried out a cake as part of the celebration, and Doug tried to get wrapped up in the joy of the moment.

He couldn't. There was still too much to say. To work out.

And then, forty-two and a half minutes later, TJ emerged from the house. It took him a sleepy second to figure out there was an impromptu party going on. Then his gaze found Doug's.

Doug held his breath as his best friend, his lover, walked across the yard to him. He actually clenched his fists in preparation. If TJ said one thing, said one single word about what they shared being wrong, he wouldn't be held accountable for his actions.

He'd spent too many hours of last night and today imagining all of TJ's excuses for walking away from him and Rosalia, and he'd worked himself up into quite a lather. Maybe he should speak first and warn TJ to tread lightly. He was a man on the edge.

In the end, words weren't necessary.

TJ walked right up to him and, in front of Doug's entire family, he kissed him. A serious, open-mouthed, no-mistaking-what-the-fuck-this-is-all-about kiss.

The entire yard—which had previously been ear-piercingly filled with laughter and talking and Leah playing the guitar—suddenly went quiet.

When they broke apart, TJ looked around. "Where's Rosalia?"

"Arkansas. Twister," Doug said, feeling slightly light-headed. What the fuck was going on?

"What? You let her chase one of those goddamn storms alone? Are you crazy? Where's your head?"

Doug had intended to be the aggressor in this facedown with TJ. The tide had turned in seconds and now he was on the defensive. "You fucking left us, Third. No note, no call, nothing."

"I was going to call, but I lost my phone."

Doug shook his head, not about to let TJ off with that excuse. "Fuck that. We were right there in bed when Sawyer called. All you had to do was wake us up and tell us what was going on. Why didn't you?"

TJ rocked back on his heels and rubbed his chin. When he didn't answer, Doug knew he'd scored a point.

Upper hand to me.

It was TJ's silence before he left that had caused him the most angst, had him questioning what they were to each other. TJ's kiss seemed to indicate that if he had been wavering in Oklahoma, he no longer was.

"I shouldn't have left like that," TJ said.

"You're right. You shouldn't have." Doug forced himself to ask the question that had been eating at him since TJ left. "You were walking away from us, weren't you?"

"I was in a bad place for a few hours." TJ glanced around the yard. "Your family showed me what a fool I've been. *You* showed me. Doug," TJ paused, and Doug could see he was fighting some pretty heavy emotions. "I went to the cemetery. You were right. About everything."

Every drop of anger that Doug felt dissolved in an instant. "I'm glad you went."

"I didn't give him a choice," Jade hollered from somewhere behind him.

Doug laughed. "Dammit, Jade. A little privacy?"

James walked over and slapped him on the back. "Kind of hard when you two are putting it all out there in the middle of the yard."

James stretched his hand out to TJ, and the two of them shook. "Welcome to the family, bro. Not that you weren't already in it. Just nice to make it all official."

TJ smiled. "Thanks. Speaking of official, I saw the drawing of the tat."

Doug glanced over at Vaughn, who shrugged. "He snuck up on me."

Laughing, Doug turned back to TJ. "What did you think?"

"I'm getting one too."

Every word TJ spoke drove Doug's anxieties from the past few hours even further into the background. TJ was in. Committed. So much so, he was going to ink it on his body.

Doug placed his hand on his lover's forearm. "We'll go together to get them. Maybe we can even talk Rosie into getting one."

Speaking her name took TJ right back to his original complaint. "You sent our Rosalia out alone," he repeated to Doug.

"She's going to be okay, man. I told Justin and Eric to look after her."

TJ rolled his eyes. "Oh, well. I'm a fool for being worried then. You've got the kittens guarding the bank."

"Fine. If it'll set your mind at ease, I'll call her right now." Doug had his cell in his hand, knowing TJ wouldn't relax until he was sure she was safe. Doug felt the same, but three years with the team had given him a stronger sense of confidence in Rosalia's abilities and the precautions she took.

No sooner had he dialed the phone than the sound of an approaching vehicle caught his attention. He grinned as Rosalia's big-ass RV rolled into view.

"Thank God," TJ muttered.

His father walked over, stepping between him and TJ as they watched Rosalia park the RV in front of the main house and step out.

"I assume this is the scientist," Dad said as Rosalia glanced around and noticed the party. She stood next to the RV, searching for them in the crowd.

Doug raised his hand and waved, capturing her attention. "That's her. That's our Rosie."

"Ours, hmm?"

TJ looked at him. "Yes, sir. I realize that probably comes as a surprise to you, and I hope—"

"Son," Dad said. "Have you taken a look around at our family dynamics? Love is love. It's as simple as that. You two have been thick as thieves for more years than I can count. I'm glad you found your happiness together. And..." He stepped forward as Rosalia approached them, stretching out his hand. "This must be the lady storm chaser."

Rosalia smiled, her ever-present blush blossoming full force. "Don't know about that description this season. No tornadoes and very few storms. The weather has been very uncooperative the last few months."

"Tell me about it," Bryant said, coming over to them. He'd just spent the entire summer dealing with drought while waiting to test the new irrigation system he'd installed on the ranch. No rain, no test. It had been a rough few months for his cousin as his doctorate had been in Mother Nature's hands, and she hadn't played nice.

Rosalia reached out to hug him. "Hey, Bryant. Long time, no see. I read all about your irrigation system. Very cool."

"Thanks. Just got the news today from the committee. I'm a doctor now, too."

Her eyes widened. "That's fantastic."

Bryant gestured around at the large gathering of family. "Hence the celebration."

"My family did the same for me except it was held in our Italian restaurant, where we drank cases of wine and ate a hundred pounds of tiramisu."

"Sounds like a damn fine party," his dad said.

"Rosie, this is my dad, Seth." And then, as if by magic, his mother emerged. "And Jody, my mom."

She shook their hands, exchanging pleasantries. Doug turned around and considered introducing everyone else but figured that would take too long and be way too overwhelming, so instead, he just said, "And this is the rest of the Compton clan."

Rosalia waved. "I've heard a lot about all of you."

"So no tornado?" TJ asked, seeking confirmation.

She shook her head. "Whole thing petered out by the time we got to Arkansas, so I grabbed a few hours of sleep, then headed here. Justin and Eric set up camp in Fayetteville. I'll meet up with them there in a few days. Are you okay? I heard about your dad and the fire."

TJ looked at Doug, and he could read the question there. Doug shook his head to reassure his friend that he hadn't told her anything about Thorn's alcoholism.

"He's fine. I know you just got here, but are you too tired to take a walk? I'd like to talk to you and Doug alone."

Rosalia nodded slowly, concern creeping into her pretty eyes. Doug reached out to give her hand a reassuring squeeze.

"We can mosey down to the creek." Doug kept hold of her hand and TJ grabbed the other. They made their way to the edge of the yard. Dusk had arrived, so Doug pulled out his cell phone and used it to light their way to the water, where they all sat down on a grassy bank.

TJ picked up a couple of small stones and tossed them in.

"TJ?" she prompted. "What do you want to talk about?"

"My dad is an alcoholic, Rosalia. He's been in and out of jail for drunk in public and driving intoxicated. He set the house on fire because he passed out with a cigarette in his mouth."

She twisted toward him, running a comforting hand along his cheek. "Oh my God! I'm so sorry. I had no idea."

TJ grimaced. "I know. Honestly, I'm not sure why I found it so hard to tell you. I guess after hearing about what happened to your grandfather, I wasn't sure how you would feel about…"

She frowned. "About what? Your dad wasn't driving the car that killed my grandfather, TJ."

"No, but he could have been. It could just as easily have been Thorn behind the wheel, leaving your grandmother or some other woman a widow."

"And that would have been on *him*, not you."

"That's what I've been telling him," Doug mumbled.

"I promised my mom I would look after him, take care of him. He's always had alcoholic tendencies."

"Didn't you tell me you were eleven when she died?" Rosalia asked.

TJ nodded.

"Jesus. Considering what you've told me about your mother, I'm very sure she didn't mean for you to wear your dad's sins as your own."

TJ ran his hand through his hair. "I know that. It's just, I've always sort of seen Thorn as my responsibility. Which hasn't been easy. He's not a nice guy."

"That's an understatement."

TJ chuckled at Doug's muttered comment. "I never thought it was fair to saddle someone else with him. I couldn't just write him off because of that promise to my mom." He gave Doug a rueful grin. "Even if he is a dick."

"Third—" Doug started.

"No. Hear me out. That's over. He's going to have to spend a lot of time in rehabilitation. He was badly injured in the fire. Beyond that, I'm not really sure where he'll end up, but that's all on him. I'm twenty-three and not making my life decisions based on him anymore. I want to be with the two of you. For as long as it lasts. Forever, if you'll have me."

"If we'll have you?" Rosalia asked with a smile that told him he was crazy to doubt it.

Doug was more interested in the last part. "Forever sounds pretty good."

Rosalia threw her hands up, though it was obvious she didn't have a problem in the world with what they were aiming for. "It's only been six weeks, guys. Do all cowboys move this fast?"

"When it's right, they do," Doug said. "We're not saying let's get hitched tomorrow—"

Rosalia laughed. "Good thing. Since it's illegal for the three of us to get married."

Doug reached over and ruffled her hair. "Smart-ass. You'll just marry one of us legally."

TJ pointed to him. "You'll marry Doug. I'm homeless and buried in debt."

Rosalia glanced from TJ to Doug and back again. "Let's table the wedding talk until we sort out the other seventy-two million things in our way."

"What things?" Doug asked.

Rosalia started counting off on her fingers. "I'll give you six big ones. My brothers."

Doug winced. "Excellent point. But there's a simple solution. We never travel east of the Mississippi. Next?"

Rosalia laughed loudly. "Fine. Three more." She pointed to herself. "My job." Then to him, "Your job." And then she tilted her head toward TJ, "And his job."

"I don't have a job," TJ added. "So that's another issue altogether."

Rosalia narrowed her gaze on TJ. "I can't have you losing your shit every time *Twister* comes on TV. That *is* my job."

TJ crinkled his nose. "Can't make any promises there."

"Third," Doug said. "You might have to try a little harder to understand what it is Rosie does."

"I know. I do think you're amazing, and as long as I'm close by when you're filming…"

Doug brightened up, remembering something he'd forgotten until that second. "Actually. Remind me to tell you about the email I got from The Weather Channel today."

The station wanted to option the rights to *Light as Air*. Which meant they all three had jobs, working together, to film and produce the show—if TJ could overcome his overprotectiveness. But there was time to talk about all of that later. He had something else in mind at the moment.

Rosalia and TJ both looked at him curiously.

"What email?" TJ asked. At the same time, Rosalia said, "The Weather Channel?"

"They want the show."

"Why would they contact you and not Rosalia?" TJ asked.

Doug chuckled. "Because I'm the producer, of course." Obviously, the studio bigwigs took the ending credits more seriously than their ragtag research team.

Rosalia feigned a shudder. "Oh my God. Does that mean Justin is really a director now?"

Doug shook his head emphatically. "Hell no. But let's talk about it later. After."

"After what?" Rosalia asked.

Doug grasped her, pulling her over his lap, facing him. "After you finish this damn list so we can have sex."

"List?" she teased. "What list?"

TJ chuckled. "We might have a small problem with that plan, Doug. My house is a pile of rubble and there's no way I'm getting it on in your parents' house."

"We all fit in the RV bed," Rosalia reminded him.

Doug glanced back toward the ranch where he could still hear the faint sounds of music and see the glow from the bonfire. "Come on. I want you to meet my brother and sister and cousins. Much as I can't wait to crawl between the sheets with you two, I feel the need to do a bit of celebrating myself."

Chapter Twelve

Rosalia glanced at her phone and marveled at the late hour…and the fact she was still awake. She'd gotten on the road at dawn this morning and driven straight to Wyoming. Then she'd met Doug's family, partied her ass off—Doug's aunts could put down some margaritas—and she sort of thought she might be unofficially engaged. To not one, but two sexy-as-sin cowboys.

What a day!

And it wasn't over, considering the hungry expressions on her handsome men's faces.

"You're still dressed," Doug said.

"I've been in this RV a total of thirty seconds."

He shook his head as if disappointed. "That's what I'm saying."

"It's time for bed. I want both of you naked. Now." TJ was leaning against the doorway to her room, waiting with less patience than Doug. She shivered at his deep-voiced demand.

The three of them had been together countless times—and ways—in the past six weeks. She couldn't help but wonder why most people didn't give ménages a try. So many delicious options.

Doug grasped her hand and dragged her to the bedroom. Once they were there, he turned her until her knees hit the mattress and she fell to her back. He was on top of her within seconds, kissing her as if they'd been apart for years instead of a single day.

As they kissed, his hands were everywhere, slipping beneath her shirt, dragging down her bra, pinching her nipples.

With one red-hot kiss, he'd not only rendered her completely sober, he'd ensured she was wide awake, so energized she could run a marathon at this point.

Her eyes flew open when Doug stilled, his lips moving away. She saw TJ standing next to them, his hand on Doug's back. At some point, while she'd been occupied, he'd taken off all his clothes.

"Oh yeah," she whispered.

"Give our girl a chance to breathe, bro."

"Damn, man." Doug pushed up, kneeling above her. His gaze, like hers, was locked on TJ's impressive erection.

They shared one quick glance at each other, then moved as a unit.

"Fuck," TJ gritted out, when Rosalia wrapped her mouth around the head of his dick as Doug palmed his balls.

His hands flew to the backs of their heads as he fisted their hair and controlled the action, pushing and pulling them according to his needs. Neither she nor Doug had a problem handing the reins to TJ. He was more than capable of driving both of them out of their minds simultaneously.

Though Doug had told TJ he wouldn't always be on top, he hadn't followed through on that threat. It appeared they'd found their natural roles with each other right out of the gate. TJ loved fucking Doug, and

Doug loved being fucked. They hadn't ruled out switching it up somewhere down the line, but for now, they both enjoyed the current status quo.

As for her, Rosalia loved watching them fuck as much as she enjoyed being on the receiving end of their affections. They so obviously cared for each other. It warmed her heart to see them together and made her love them both even more.

Rosalia stilled at the thought.

TJ, ever astute, noticed. "Rosalia."

She released him with a soft pop, peering up at him. None of them had said the words yet. It occurred to her now that they'd been waiting. Waiting for TJ to make that final leap—either to them or away from them.

Rosalia hadn't even realized it until this moment. Somewhere in her subconscious, she'd recognized that he'd been holding back. That reticence was completely gone now.

She was free to speak her feelings.

"I love you," she said to TJ.

She saw him swallow deeply before the sexiest, sweetest smile she'd ever been graced with flashed bright. "I love you, too, darlin'. So much it almost hurts."

Rosalia turned her attention to Doug, not bothering to wipe away the happy tears clouding her vision. "I love you, too."

Doug pressed his forehead to hers, both of them closing their eyes. "You're my everything, Rosie. You and TJ are my world. I don't know how I lived a day without you. And I hope I never have to figure that out."

TJ lifted her shirt over her head, then quickly unfastened her bra. She didn't feel the urge to cover

176

herself anymore. That shyness was gone when she was with them.

She stood briefly, slipping off her jeans, before sitting back down on the bed. Rosalia leaned back, inviting TJ to join her. He gave her a sexy grin as he followed, coming over her, kissing her.

Doug watched as he stripped off his own clothing before settling down next to them. She felt his hand on her hip, softly caressing as TJ kissed her stupid.

Sometimes she wondered if this constant state of breathless light-headedness was healthy. The lack of oxygen getting to her brain ensured she didn't worry about that for too long.

"Open your legs, darlin'. I need to be inside you."

She was used to long, drawn-out foreplay with her men, and while she loved every minute of that, she wasn't going to complain about a quickie either.

Rosalia wrapped her legs around TJ's waist, her breath catching as he slid into her in one smooth, steady glide.

Her eyes drifted shut in bliss. There was nothing like the feeling of being filled by TJ...or Doug. She'd spent so many years alone, without this closeness. Even now, she wondered how she'd managed to get through all those long, dreary, nothing-special days.

TJ lifted his hips, slowly sliding out before returning. She was used to him taking her harder, deeper. Tonight, he was steady and patient, something she'd never noticed in him.

That thought prompted a grin that caught his eye.

"What?"

"As much as I love the gentle motion of the ocean, I'm a storm-chasing girl at heart."

TJ chuckled. "Tough shit. I want to make love to my future wife. There will be no tornado-force fucking tonight."

She crinkled her nose as if disappointed, even as her heart nearly burst with joy when he said future wife.

"I want to be a part of this," Doug murmured.

TJ glanced over at his friend. "I think you should be." And then, with one smooth, swift motion, Rosalia found herself on top, astride TJ.

Doug's hand was on her ass in an instant, stroking the cheeks as he bent down to place a kiss at the base of her spine. "Both of us, Rosie. You're taking both of us."

She nodded, excitedly. They'd never done this before, but she'd dreamed of it, even suggested it one night a few weeks ago. Doug and TJ had declared her too inexperienced for something like that at the time.

"Not just into your body," Doug continued. "But into your life."

"And my heart," she added, wanting both of them to know that she got it. She felt it. She wanted it more than she'd ever wanted anything in her life.

Doug rummaged through the nightstand drawer for the nearly empty tube of lubrication there.

"We need to make a trip to the store," he murmured, prompting laughter from Rosalia and TJ.

"We should probably buy stock in KY," TJ joked.

Rosalia's giggle was cut short when he squeezed some of the lube inside her anus. She sucked in a lungful of air, then held her breath as he pressed one, two…God…three fingers inside.

She lifted her hips, TJ slipping out as she sought more from Doug.

When TJ placed a sharp slap on her upper thigh, reminding her where she was supposed to be, she resumed her previous position, taking him back inside, buried to the hilt.

Doug stretched her ass for a few minutes more before donning a condom.

"Ready?" he asked.

She nodded, too aroused to speak.

Neither she nor TJ moved as he slowly made his way into the tight portal.

Rosalia trembled slightly, her need growing painful. It was always this way. Both men took their time, prepared her body to accept them. She was grateful for that, but at the same time, she felt savage, turning into a primitive beast who wanted to be taken roughly.

TJ gripped her hips, holding her still as if he could read her desires. He knew she was on the verge of going wild.

Once Doug was fully seated, he also held still for just a moment.

Her gaze was locked on TJ's face, *his* eyes focused on Doug. She was used to her lovers communicating without words. She didn't have a clue what tacit agreement they'd just come to, but the dark, hungry look on TJ's face told her she was in for one hell of a night.

TJ's hands shifted to her breasts, squeezing them gently at first before adding more pressure.

Doug's hands took over on her hips, holding her in place.

"Please," she whispered when neither man moved.

"Tell us what you want, Rosalia," TJ said.

"We'll give you anything," Doug promised.

"I want hard and fast and deep and..." Her words fell away because they didn't need to hear more.

One second she was giving them a grocery list of fantasy words, and the next, they were fulfilling them.

TJ's hips lifted as Doug retreated. While the concept of threesomes had been new to all of them, it hadn't taken them long to find the sweet spots.

Within seconds, they'd found their rhythm, and she realized her desires weren't just hers. They were shared.

Doug kept calling out her name as his fingers tightened on her hips, tugging her ass toward his cock as he slammed in harder.

TJ pinched her nipples, increasing the pressure until she cried from the pleasure and the pain. He was a master of provoking so many contrasting, beautiful sensations.

Rosalia's first orgasm shook her hard, but her lovers ignored it. They weren't even close to finished yet. Two hard cocks continued to pound as she soared into orbit, disintegrating in an explosion of blinding white light and ear-piercing thunder.

When she floated back to earth, they were still there, taking her, claiming her. Mere seconds passed before her body went up and over again.

It didn't matter to Doug or TJ, and that was when it occurred to her that she wasn't the only rabid creature in the room.

She raked her fingernails down TJ's chest, scoring his skin, leaving her mark. He hissed, pinching her nipples again before gripping the back of her head and pressing her lips down to his. He nipped the lower one, and she tasted the salty tang of blood. She reciprocated in kind. TJ's eyes narrowed, then closed as he groaned.

"Fuck, Rosalia. My love, my beautiful love."

Doug's fingers dug deeper into her hips. "I can't...God...I want..."

"Do it," TJ commanded through gritted teeth.

Doug stiffened, his cock fully encased in the tightness of her ass. He jerked roughly as he came, a myriad of curses falling from his lips.

"Mother of fucking God. Holy Christ!"

Rosalia soaked up the words, tried to focus on each burst of come as she imagined it filling the condom. It was that or fall off the cliff again, and she seriously wasn't sure she was strong enough to recover from another orgasm like the first two.

As Doug's climax waned, he withdrew. Rosalia started to sigh, missing him as much as she was grateful for the reprieve.

That feeling was short-lived when TJ flipped her to her back and started thrusting inside her like a man possessed.

Her back arched, his hard, forceful entry driving her to an orgasm she never saw coming. She screamed, unaware of it until Doug's hand covered her mouth. His response brought her back to reality for a split second, just long enough to remember her RV was parked right outside his family's house.

That thought was fleeting, because TJ obviously didn't give a shit *who* heard what they were doing. He bent his head to her breast and sucked her nipple into his mouth—hard.

She gasped, her hands gripping his hair, torn between pulling him away and holding him close.

"Fuck me harder," she demanded.

TJ lifted his head, his breath coming out in loud, panting gasps. He looked at her for just a moment before withdrawing.

She didn't have a chance to complain before he'd flipped her to her stomach. TJ was the only person she'd ever met with the ability to make her feel like a rag doll. It was a huge fucking turn-on.

He lifted her hips and slammed back into her pussy from behind. Clever devil knew that was the one sure way to find her G-spot. He hit it in one.

She turned her face toward the pillow, letting it absorb the next scream as he thrust in hard and fast.

Rosalia felt as if she'd been swept up in a tornado, light as air. Wild. Free. She was being ravaged—and she loved every second of it.

She came again, and this time, thank God, TJ was there with her, filling her with spurt after spurt of hot come.

She wanted babies.

It was the only lucid thought she could produce as her body shuddered in the aftermath of all they'd done.

She shook violently one last time as TJ pulled out, dropping to her side. Doug had already claimed the other, watching them intently, if somewhat drowsily. They teased him about how quickly he fell asleep after coming.

At some point, probably when TJ was fucking her senseless, he'd disposed of the condom.

"I want babies."

She hadn't meant to say that aloud.

"Right now?" Doug asked. At the same time, TJ said, "You got it."

She giggled, surprised she could find the breath for that response. "Sorry. Guess that came out of left field."

TJ rolled to face her, placing his palm over her stomach. "Maybe so, but I'm not complaining about where your head is at the moment. I've basically been alone since my mom died. I want a family too."

Doug placed his hand on top of TJ's. "You've got one, Third. You've got us."

"And we're going to make babies," she repeated, the idea seriously stuck. Probably because they'd fucked her senseless and left her with just one little brain cell.

"Yeah," Doug said softly. "A shy little girl who blushes like her mother. We'll name her Janet, after your mom, TJ."

TJ nodded, and Rosalia was touched by the wetness that appeared on his lashes. "She would have liked that."

"So much for making love, Third," Rosalia teased. Doug's infectious sense of humor had rubbed off on her. "That was definitely a category five."

TJ groaned, the sound a cross between a chuckle and genuine anguish. "Between the storm chasing and the sex, you two will be the death of me."

Doug yawned. "Pretty sure my folks heard those screams of yours, Rosie. Going to be embarrassing at the breakfast table tomorrow. My mom promised to make us all French toast."

Rosalia giggled. "Next time, we'll park the RV farther away from the house."

"A state away should work," TJ suggested. "Speaking of category fives, Rosalia, how do you feel about tattoos?"

Epilogue

Silas relaxed, kicked back in the chair, boots crossed at his ankles, as he stared at the flames of the campfire. The sound of a can cracking open told him Seth had grabbed another beer from the cooler. It was still early spring, but they'd had some unseasonably warm weather this past week and it had Silas itching to get outside in the fresh air.

After a damn cold winter, it felt like he'd been hibernating for months. He'd been working in the barn when it occurred to him, he and his brothers hadn't been camping alone in years. Scratch that, it had been decades.

When they were just young bucks—in their teens and early twenties—they'd often saddled up the horses with their tents, sleeping bags, hot dogs and a case or two of beer, and spent a night together under the stars.

He wasn't sure what it was that had made him long to make the trip again, but the second he suggested it to his brothers, they'd been all for it. Within hours, they'd loaded up the horses and were on their way to "their spot."

Lucy had tried to pack them up some kind of fancy campfire food packets she'd read about online, but he'd insisted a big pile of hot dogs, buns and couple of onions were just fine.

"Quite a winter," Sawyer said, as soon as he polished off his third—or maybe fourth—hot dog. "Started to think we were at the beginning of another Ice Age there for a little while."

"I hear you," Seth agreed. "Feels good to be out here without long johns and wool socks."

Sam nodded, his gaze resting on Silas. "It does, but I suspect it's not just the unseasonably nice weather that has us out here. What's up, Si? You got something on your mind?"

Sam, the college boy, was always the most astute. Sawyer and Seth were more like him, physical guys with a love of nature, horses, sunrises and sunsets. Sam appreciated those things too, but he liked to attach meaning to it all.

Silas didn't mind the question because he'd been pondering the reason as well. "Just been thinking lately about our camping trips when we were younger. Feels like we've traveled a million miles since then."

Seth chuckled. "Probably more like a hundred million. We're getting damn old."

Silas couldn't argue with that. "Tell me about it. Woke up the other day, took a look in the mirror and saw JD staring back at me."

Sawyer grinned. "You *are* starting to look a lot like our old man, Si. Leah pointed it out to me a few months ago. It's the graying hair and those deep lines around your eyes and mouth."

Silas harrumphed. "The wrinkles, you mean. Those are what happen when you have kids. Must've told Lucy and Colby a thousand times when Hope and Austin were growing up, we should have just gotten a couple of house cats and called it good enough."

Seth took a big swig of beer. "Seems kind of strange to be on the other side of all that, doesn't it? My kids worried the hell out of me when they were younger. Now…I've been thinking about JD and Vicky a lot lately. Thinking about how they must have felt after all of us were hitched up. Especially as I've watched James and Sienna and Doug fall in love and settle down, watched Sienna become a mother and seen how she raises her own kids. You spend so much time worrying about them when they're young, then holding your breath as they become adults and get their hearts stomped on a few dozen times, always hoping they'll bounce back and find their footing again. Lately, I just look at who they've become and think, how the hell did I manage to raise these three amazing people?"

Sawyer, ever the joker, reached for the big bag of chips at his feet and popped one in his mouth. "You didn't do that. Jody did. Jody and good genes."

Seth chucked one of Hope's homemade chocolate chip cookies at Sawyer, who caught it just before it smacked him in the face and took a big bite.

Silas tossed another log on the fire. "We gave our folks a run for their money too when we were younger. Four arrogant pups who thought they knew everything."

Sam snorted. "We didn't know a damn thing back then."

"You can say that again." Seth tugged off his hat, toying with the brim. "I hope JD would have been as proud of our kids as I am."

"He would have been." There wasn't a hint of doubt in Sam's voice.

Silas agreed. "Hell, he'd have been over the moon with that lot, riding in that big rig with Austin on his runs."

"So he could brag about his grandson Bryant's amazing irrigation system," Sam added. "He'd be preaching that to ranches all over the country like the gospel."

Sawyer chuckled. "And twenty buck says he would have wanted to jump out of a plane into one of James's fires or chase one of Doug's tornadoes."

Silas rubbed his chin. "I miss him."

None of the others replied, though they all nodded.

"And Jake," Sam added after a minute or so. "Been a rough year without him. Didn't realize how much I relied on that guy. Still catch myself walking out to the barn or to his cabin at least two or three times a week to talk to him."

"I do the same thing," Seth admitted.

Silas cleared the lump forming in his throat. "That's how life works. Old ones die, young ones fall in love, babies come along. One big compass directing us down a million different paths at once, yet somehow…"

"They all lead us back home," Seth added.

Silas nodded slowly. His brothers got it. They always got it. And it seemed they'd all been able to impart the same lessons JD and Vicky and Jake had passed on to them to their own kids.

Compass Ranch was home.

Their home.

And it always would be.

***

We hope you enjoyed the last Compass book! While it's very sad to leave the Comptons forever, don't despair! Meet the Collins clan. Now is a great time to check out Mari's latest series, Wilder Irish, featuring a big Baltimore family, sexy heroes, and smart, sassy heroines. January Girl is available now!

Join Mari's newsletter and Jayne's Naughty News so you don't miss new releases, contests, or exclusive subscriber-only content.

Be sure to read on for a very special letter from Mari and Jayne to Compass fans and if you are on

Facebook, come join the fun on the Compass Series Page.

Read on for an excerpt from Mari's book, January Girl.

She's sleeping with the enemy...

"I think perhaps you should move on. The lady told you it's over."

Caitlyn was startled when Lucas decided to enter the conversation. She assumed he would move on at the first sign of Sammy's drama. For some strange reason, knowing he was there allowed her to calm down. While she was fairly certain her punch wouldn't leave a mark, Lucas Whiting looked the type to do some serious damage to Sammy. Which was exactly what she wanted.

"Who are you?" Sammy kept his tone fairly non-confrontational. Probably because he was smart enough to take one look at Lucas and know he wouldn't win in a physical fight against the man.

"I'll tell you who I am. I'm your worst nightmare if you don't get out of this pub and leave this woman alone."

Sammy blinked a couple times, no doubt trying to figure out if he'd heard what he thought he'd heard. Dumbass actually looked at her for help, and it took all the strength she had not to roll her eyes.

"Go home, Sammy. Don't come back."

The air seemed to seep out of him as Sammy held her gaze a second longer. And then, he turned to leave.

She twisted back toward Lucas, grinning despite her annoyance with basically everything at the moment. "What the hell was that? It was like you were channeling Liam Neeson or something for a second. I will find you. I'm your worst nightmare," she mimicked in a deep, deadly voice.

Lucas didn't look her way, didn't even acknowledge her joke. Instead, he continued to watch Sammy's retreating form.

Caitlyn saw her ex walk out of the pub. Then she glanced toward the bar. Very little happened that Uncle Tris didn't see or hear. He stared at her for a second. She gave him a covert wink to let him know she was fine. Regardless, his face remained stoic before he gave her a subtle nod.

He was going to leave her alone. For now. But she didn't fool herself into believing he wasn't going to be watching her like a hawk as long as she was talking to Lucas Whiting.

"Thank you for stepping in to help," she said, her gaze slipping to the door to her apartment. She was so close. To pajamas and a glass of wine and repeats of Lucifer on TV.

"Is my chivalry enough to convince you to join me for a drink?"

She glanced back at his table, surprised to find it unoccupied. "What happened to your friends?"

"They're business associates. And our meeting is over. They've gone home to their wives."

He gestured toward a chair and she gave in. Tiredness gave way to curiosity.

"No wife for you?"

He shook his head. "Would I invite you for a drink if there was?"

"The idiot you just kicked out of here was coming home to me after work. When he beat me there, he decided it would be a good idea to invite another woman to our bed. You'll forgive me if I'm not super trusting."

"I'm not married. Not engaged. Not living with or seriously dating anyone."

Caitlyn found herself trying to figure out Lucas's age. He had one of those faces that made it virtually impossible to guess. Not that she'd have to wonder for long. No doubt there was plenty of information about him on the Internet. She could discover that answer in one quick Google search on her phone.

"Divorced?" she asked.

"No."

She realized they'd sort of started this conversation in the middle, so she thought she'd try to drag them back a few steps to the beginning. "I'm Caitlyn Wallace, by the way."

His expression gave her no clue as to whether or not he recognized her name. If he'd done any research at all on the pub, he would have certainly come across her mother's name.

Pop Pop and her grandma Sunday had raised their seven children in the upstairs apartment Caitlyn was sharing with her cousins, in addition to running the pub and restaurant below. As they became adults, Tris took over the pub half of the business with Pop Pop while her mom, Keira Wallace, and Uncle Ewan ran Sunday's Side.

"Lucas Whiting."

"I know."

For the first time, she saw just the trace of a smile on his face. It made him appear almost human.

"The man who just left—"

"Sammy," she added.

"Former boyfriend or husband?"

"Ex-boyfriend. It's been a small consolation knowing that at least I was smart enough not to marry him."

"He asked?"

She shook her head. "Actually, no. He didn't."

Sammy was the last thing Caitlyn wanted to talk about tonight. Especially with Lucas Whiting. "Do you do a lot of business in pubs?"

Lucas lifted one shoulder casually. "Depends on the business."

Hello, Mr. Vague. She probed for more. "Okay. So what was tonight's pub-worthy business?"

"Real estate acquisition."

Fucker was good. He gave nothing away.

"Can I get you all something to drink?" Ailis was looking at Caitlyn curiously.

"I'll have another Guinness. Caitlyn?"

"I'll have the same. Thanks." She hoped her cousin wouldn't say anything to reveal her identity. The lawyer in her was determined to get to the truth in Lucas's short answers.

Ailis paused for just a second, but when Caitlyn didn't look at her or say more, she turned for the bar.

"I can't imagine there's much real estate left in Baltimore your family doesn't already own."

Lucas's gaze held hers intently. "There's always more to buy."

His response tweaked her for some reason.

"What if someone doesn't want to sell to you?"

His eyes narrowed the tiniest bit. Someone who was paying less attention wouldn't have even noticed, but Caitlyn had locked onto him. Her words had triggered something. Shit. She'd shown her hand. Revealed herself.

"Everyone has a price."

Her family didn't. Not when it came to this business. It wasn't just the Collins's livelihood. It was their home, their legacy to future generations. In some ways, the pub felt like the heartbeat of the family, the one thing that kept them all tied together.

"So no one has ever said no to you?"

For the first time, Lucas grinned. Caitlyn's response shook her. She was torn between running away from the hungry wolf and baring her neck to the beast.

Oh shit.

He leaned closer to her, his dark eyes penetrating, missing nothing. His expression seemed to say he knew she wouldn't say no to him.

Her pussy clenched, and she felt a trickle of wetness between her legs. What the hell was going on? Lucas shot one sexy freaking look at her and she was ready to tear off her clothes? It was definitely time to start dating again. Her hormones had decided to make a comeback…with a vengeance.

She tried to imagine what Lucas would look like without his shirt on. Did he have any tattoos? His thick, muscular arms seemed made for ink.

"What do you think?" he murmured.

About the tattoos? It took her a moment to stop undressing him with her eyes and recall her original question.

She'd asked if anyone ever said no to him.

"I don't know." She hated the almost breathless quality in her voice.

Her cheeks heated under his intense gaze, and she feared she was blushing. Lucas wasn't even bothering to hide his attraction to her. His eyes darted down to her breasts, and the shadow of his grin reappeared.

She averted her eyes when it became impossible to hide her own unwanted desires. Unfortunately, looking down only made it apparent that her nipples were poking through her blouse. They'd tightened the moment she sat down at the table and gotten a whiff of his musk cologne. Which meant Lucas knew exactly what effect he was having on her.

"People say no to me all the time, Caitlyn."

Her gaze lifted as she wondered if she would have the strength to deny him. In her mind, she could imagine him bidding her to strip, to kneel, to bend over the table. And she didn't doubt for a second she would comply. "People," she murmured. "Women?" The question slipped out unbidden.

Lucas parted his lips to speak, but she shook her head to cut him off.

"I didn't mean...never mind." She was babbling like an idiot. Time to get her shit together. "When people say no, when they turn down your offer, do you walk away?"

Lucas looked like he wanted to respond to her foolish slip of the tongue. She was grateful when she let her attempt to return them to safer ground stick. He tilted his head. "I never walk away. As I said, there's always a bottom line."

Caitlyn tried to recall the last time she'd felt this far out of her league. Years spent in her legal practice had honed her skills, her ability to stand up to even the most vicious of bullies. The problem was Lucas didn't strike her as a bully.

He felt more like—she swallowed heavily—a Dom.

And she was terrified he'd find a way to look deep inside her and see the one thing she really did not want Lucas Whiting to see.

Her mother had told her once that the worst thing a person could do was hide their true personality, to deny who they were, to try to conceal the one thing that made them beautiful, made them special.

Her mother knew who Caitlyn was. She knew it because they were the same underneath the skin. Mom had always seen, always tried to encourage Caitlyn in very subtle ways to accept her submissiveness. To embrace it and not view it as a weakness.

Caitlyn continually struggled with that acceptance, and she'd never had any difficulty keeping the trait hidden from pretty much everyone.

Until now.

The problem was Lucas was looking at her too closely. His body language, his carriage, the way he held himself, God, everything about him was luring her closer to the fire.

She pressed her legs together tightly, desperate to stop the sudden pulsing of her inner muscles that were screaming for sex. She needed to get a grip, needed to break free of…whatever this was. Lucas Whiting was the enemy, a threat to her family's livelihood. The thought of her family helped her find her bearings.

"I disagree about the bottom line. Some things simply can't be bought. For any price."

Lucas didn't bother to argue with her. His cool expression made it perfectly clear he thought he was right and she was wrong. His haughty attitude tweaked her.

"What do you do for a living, Caitlyn?"

"I'm a lawyer."

"Criminal or civil?"

"Civil. I have my own practice." She'd nearly said the name of her firm, but stopped short. Lucas might not recognize the name Wallace, but there was no way in hell he didn't know the Collins family owned this pub.

"Large firm?"

"No. Small. Just my cousin and I, though recently we've started putting out feelers, looking to expand, perhaps add another attorney or two."

"So business is good."

"Yes. It is. We work with lower-income families, senior citizens."

"I see."

"I primarily deal with property disputes, landlord and tenant issues, immigration. My cousin works more with divorce and child-custody type cases."

"So you're not ambulance chasers."

She shook her head and grinned. "No. We're not."

Ailis returned and placed their pints of beer on the table. Tris must have clued her cousin into the fact that Caitlyn was up to something, because she simply said she'd check on them in a bit and moved on to deliver drinks to the table next to them.

If they were counting on Caitlyn for information, they were going to be sorely disappointed. She was striking out. Big time.

She glanced toward the door to her apartment again. This game of cat and mouse had her on edge. And horny as hell.

She'd joined Lucas intent on discovering his secrets. Instead, it felt as if he was uncovering hers.

Caitlyn needed to move the conversation away from herself. Lucas was too good at dodging her questions, making her forget why he was here. "Was your meeting tonight successful? Were you able to buy what you wanted?"

"Not yet. We're in the beginning phases of the project."

"What does that involve?"

Lucas took a sip of beer and leaned back in his chair. "Research."

Caitlyn fought to control her temper—and the niggling bit of fear—his words provoked. He still wanted to buy Pat's Pub. There wasn't any doubt in her mind. What she couldn't tell was if he knew who she was, if he was baiting her, using her as part of that so-called research.

With her family's livelihood on the line, Caitlyn found herself better able to snuff out her ill-advised, unwanted attraction to Lucas. "Sounds like we're similar souls. I know quite a bit about research myself."

Her tone was more threatening than she'd intended, but she refused to cower, refused to let Lucas think he had the upper hand.

It was obvious her sudden aggression caught him off guard, making her think, once again, that he didn't have a clue who she was.

He recovered quickly. Damn him. "Tell me about yourself, Caitlyn."

She took a deep breath. Clearly, she still had a shot at trying to figure out his intentions. "I'm not sure what there is to tell. I think we pretty much covered all the bases already. I'm a lawyer. I'm single. And I have shitty taste in men."

Lucas chuckled, and she couldn't help but think it sounded rusty. Was this guy always so serious?

"I'm curious what the attraction was between you and Sammy. He doesn't seem like your type."

She frowned. "We've known each other approximately twenty minutes. How do you know what my type is?"

196

"You don't make it very far in my line of business without paying attention to details. You studied law. I study people."

Caitlyn felt compelled to push Lucas's buttons. The man seemed unshakable. Which made her long to rattle him. "You can't figure someone out in just twenty minutes."

"Sammy is weak."

She shrugged. "So?"

"So that's not what you want. What you need."

The way he said the word "need" had her chest going tight with fear…and, God help her, longing. "You have no idea what I need." She'd meant to put some power, some strength behind her assertion. Instead, the words came out in a whisper that belied them.

Once again, Lucas didn't reply. He didn't have to. How the man could say so much with just one look was beyond her, but it was obvious he knew way too much about her needs.

Lucas let his gaze travel over her body, taking his time as he studied every aspect of her. "You dress conservatively, but you know how to accentuate your strongest features. While you don't seek to hide the fact that you're very beautiful, your dress slacks, your simple silk blouse, and the understated jewelry prove that you wish to appear professional, not sexy. I assume that's something you—as a woman in a male-dominated world—have to be attuned to. You're every bit as intelligent as your male contemporaries and you are determined to be seen as such."

She shrugged, still struggling to recover from the needs he'd uncovered with just a few words and heated looks. "You've just described pretty much every woman in my profession."

"Are you daring me to dig deeper, Cait?"

She shivered at the dark tone in his voice that felt almost possessive.

She couldn't play this game anymore. Couldn't risk having him expose something she didn't want to acknowledge, especially to him. "Why are you at this pub?"

"You know why."

"Say it anyway."

"I want to buy it."

January Girl is available NOW.

Dear Readers,

When Jayne and I began writing the Compass Brothers series back in late 2010, I'm not sure either of us could have predicted where these books would take us. *Northern Exposure* released in March 2011, the story prompting our favorite review of all time as a reader wrote that the book was "so dirty, I had to read it in the dark so Jesus couldn't see me," and it's been a true adventure ever since.

So many of my fondest memories as an author are wrapped up in these stories. I can recall the night my editor, Lindsey Faber, called me and simply said, "You hit it." I didn't have a clue what she was talking about until she added, "The *New York Times*. *Eastern Ambitions* hit the list." I was halfway up the stairs in my house, and I turned around and sat down, my knees going weak. My husband found me sitting there after I said goodbye to Lindsey. He said, "What's wrong?" By that point, I was crying tears of joy, only able to choke out the words, "I hit the *New York Times* bestseller list." He's a typical man, so he looked at me as tears streamed down my face, shook his head, amused by my reaction, and said, "Call your mother."

I did. And then I called Jayne in Ohio, who I decided later was actually in very real shock and probably should have been wrapped in a blanket and taken to the emergency room. We still laugh about her monotone replies during that phone call to my screaming, "Oh my God" and "Do you believe this?!" The shock wore off after an hour or so, and then it was her turn to call me back, screaming and squealing.

I'm happy to say we were much more composed when *Western Ties* hit the list as well, just a few months later. Okay, I'm lying. We were wrecks that day too!

I remember the exact moment when JD died. I was sitting at my desk, crying so hard, I could barely see to type the words. Once again, my husband walked by, shook his head, and said, "You know these people aren't real, right?" All I could say was, "To me, they *are* real." Once it was finished, I called Jayne, who was scuba diving in some freaking exotic location, having the time of her life. I vowed revenge and got it—four books later—when I made her write the end of Vicky's story in *Falling Softly*.

With the closing of Samhain Publishing, the original home of Compass Brothers and Compass Girls, the stories came back to us. Jayne created the beautiful new covers and we decided it was time to tell the boys' stories. The plan for three four-book series had always been there, but life and other series got in the way, delaying the release of Compass Boys until last year.

I'll admit I was concerned about trying to dive back into the books after so many years, but that anxiety vanished before I'd finished the first page of the story. The voices, the characters, the world was all still there, and it felt like I'd come home to Compass Ranch after too many years away.

And now, it's time to say goodbye again. For the last time.

Jayne and I want to thank each and every one of you for taking this journey with us. Eight years, twelve books, one ranch, three deaths, sixteen sexy cowboys, tattoos aplenty, and too many wonderful memories to count...

COMPASS RULES!

All the best,
Mari

If you haven't already read the rest of the Compass saga, be sure to go back and read all the original Compass Brothers (Silas, Seth, Sam, and Sawyer) and their daughters, the Compass Girls (Sienna, Hope, Jade, and Sterling).

About the Authors

Jayne Rylon and Mari Carr met at a writing conference in June 2009 and instantly became arch enemies. Two authors couldn't be more opposite. Mari, when free of her librarian-by-day alter ego, enjoys a drink or two or...more. Jayne, allergic to alcohol, lost huge sections of her financial-analyst mind to an epic explosion resulting from Mari gloating about her hatred of math. To top it off, they both had works in progress with similar titles and their heroes shared a name. One of them would have to go.

The battle between them for dominance was a bloody but short one, when they realized they'd be better off combining their forces for good (or smut). With the ink dry on the peace treaty, they emerged as good friends, who have a remarkable amount in common despite their differences, and their writing partnership has flourished. Except for the time Mari attempted to poison Jayne with a bottle of Patron. Accident or retaliation? You decide.

Join Mari's newsletter and Jayne's Naughty News so you don't miss new releases, contests, or exclusive subscriber-only content.

Mari Carr and Jayne Rylon

Look for these titles by Mari Carr

Compass:
Northern Exposure
Southern Comfort
Eastern Ambitions
Western Ties
Winter's Thaw
Hope Springs
Summer Fling
Falling Softly
Heaven on Earth
Into the Fire
Still Waters

Second Chances:
Fix You
Dare You
Just You
Near You
Reach You
Always You

Sparks in Texas:
Sparks Fly
Waiting for You
Something Sparked
Off Limits
No Other Way
Whiskey Eyes

Trinity Masters:
Elemental Pleasure
Primal Passion
Scorching Desire

Light as Air

Forbidden Legacy
Hidden Devotion
Elegant Seduction
Secret Scandal
Delicate Ties
Beloved Sacrifice
Masterful Truth

Masters' Admiralty:
Treachery's Devotion

Wild Irish:
Come Monday
Ruby Tuesday
Waiting for Wednesday
Sweet Thursday
Friday I'm in Love
Saturday Night Special
Any Given Sunday
Wild Irish Christmas
Wild Irish Box Set

Wilder Irish:
January Girl
February Stars
March Wind
Guardian Angel

Big Easy:
Blank Canvas
Crash Point
Full Position
Rough Draft
Triple Beat
Winner Takes All

Going Too Fast

Boys of Fall:
Free Agent
Red Zone
Illegal Motion
Going Deep
Wild Card
Full Coverage
Going Hard

Clandestine:
Bound by the Past
Covert Affairs
Scoring
Mad about Meg

Cocktales:
Party Naked
Screwdriver
Bachelor's Bait
Screaming O

Farpoint Creek:
Outback Princess
Outback Cowboy
Outback Master
Outback Lovers

June Girls:
No Recourse
No Regrets

Just Because:
Because of You

Because You Love Me
Because It's True

Love Lessons:
Happy Hour
Slam Dunk

Madison Girls:
Kiss Me Kate
Three Reasons Why

Scoundrels:
Black Jack
White Knight
Red Queen

What Women Want:
Sugar and Spice
Everything Nice
What Women Want

Individual Titles:
Seducing the Boss
Erotic Research
Tequila Truth
Power Play
Rough Cut
Assume the Position
One Daring Night
Do Over

Cowboys!:
Spitfire
Rekindled
Inflamed

Mari Carr and Jayne Rylon

Cowboy Heat

Light as Air

Also By Jayne Rylon

MEN IN BLUE
Hot Cops Save Women In Danger
Night is Darkest
Razor's Edge
Mistress's Master
Spread Your Wings
Wounded Hearts
Bound For You

DIVEMASTERS
Sexy SCUBA Instructors By Day, Doms On A
Mega-Yacht By Night
Going Down
Going Deep
Going Hard

POWERTOOLS
Five Guys Who Get It On With Each Other &
One Girl. Enough Said?
Kate's Crew
Morgan's Surprise
Kayla's Gift
Devon's Pair
Nailed to the Wall
Hammer it Home

HOT RODS
Powertools Spin Off. Keep up with the Crew
plus...
Seven Guys & One Girl. Enough Said?
King Cobra
Mustang Sally
Super Nova

Mari Carr and Jayne Rylon

Rebel on the Run
Swinger Style
Barracuda's Heart
Touch of Amber
Long Time Coming

STANDALONE
Menage
4-Ever Theirs
Nice & Naughty
Contemporary
Where There's Smoke
Report For Booty

COMPASS BROTHERS
Modern Western Family Drama Plus Lots Of Steamy Sex
Northern Exposure
Southern Comfort
Eastern Ambitions
Western Ties

COMPASS GIRLS
Daughters Of The Compass Brothers Drive Their Dads Crazy And Fall In Love
Winter's Thaw
Hope Springs
Summer Fling
Falling Softly

PLAY DOCTOR
Naughty Sexual Psychology Experiments Anyone?
Dream Machine
Healing Touch

Light as Air

RED LIGHT
A Hooker Who Loves Her Job
Complete Red Light Series Boxset
FREE - Through My Window - FREE
Star
Can't Buy Love
Free For All

PICK YOUR PLEASURES
Choose Your Own Adventure Romances!
Pick Your Pleasure
Pick Your Pleasure 2

RACING FOR LOVE
MMF Menages With Race-Car Driver Heroes
Complete Series Boxset
Driven
Shifting Gears

PARANORMALS
Vampires, Witches, And A Man Trapped In A
Painting
Paranormal Double Pack Boxset
Picture Perfect
Reborn

2491

Made in the USA
Lexington, KY
15 June 2018